W9-DHF-635

*** ALL POINTS BULLETIN ***

Sheriff's Department
Jester, Montana

Late March: Be advised that Sheriff Luke McNeil has gone missing in the ice storm rapidly moving through the area. The tall, dark lawman was last seen rushing from the sheriff's office, responding to a call. Unconfirmed reports put him at the Faulkner farm. Since power lines are down and roads are treacherous due to the weather, any attempt to reach the sheriff will have to wait till morning. We can only hope that Sheriff McNeil and Ms. Faulkner will be safe together in a drafty old farmhouse with only each other to keep them warm. There's no telling how long the storm will last, but it swept in as fast and furiously as the rumored sparks between the Montana man and the lady millionaire. More details as they develop...

Dear Reader,

This month we have a wonderful lineup of stories, guaranteed to warm you on these last chilly days of winter. First, Charlotte Douglas kicks things off with *Surprise Inheritance*, the third installment in Harlequin American Romance's MILLIONAIRE, MONTANA series, in which a sexy sheriff is reunited with the woman he's always loved when she returns to town to claim her inheritance.

Next, THE BABIES OF DOCTORS CIRCLE, Jacqueline Diamond's new miniseries centered around a maternity and well-baby clinic, premieres this month with *Diagnosis: Expecting Boss's Baby*. In this sparkling story, an unforgettable night of passion between a secretary and her handsome employer leads to an unexpected pregnancy.

Also available this month is *Sweeping the Bride Away* by Michele Dunaway. A bride-to-be is all set to wed "Mr. Boring" until she hires a rugged contractor who makes her pulse race and gives her second thoughts about her upcoming nuptials. Rounding things out is *Professor & the Pregnant Nanny* by Emily Dalton. This heartwarming story pairs a single dad in need of a nanny for his three adorable children with a woman who is alone, pregnant and in need of a job.

Enjoy this month's offerings as Harlequin American Romance continues to celebrate twenty years of publishing the best in contemporary category romance fiction. Be sure to come back next month for more stories guaranteed to touch your heart!

Melissa Jeglinski
Associate Senior Editor
Harlequin American Romance

SURPRISE INHERITANCE

Charlotte Douglas

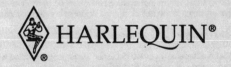

HARLEQUIN®

TORONTO • NEW YORK • LONDON
AMSTERDAM • PARIS • SYDNEY • HAMBURG
STOCKHOLM • ATHENS • TOKYO • MILAN • MADRID
PRAGUE • WARSAW • BUDAPEST • AUCKLAND

Special thanks and acknowledgment are given to
Charlotte Douglas for her contribution to the
MILLIONAIRE, MONTANA series.

ISBN 0-373-16961-2

SURPRISE INHERITANCE

Copyright © 2003 by Harlequin Books S.A.

Visit us at www.eHarlequin.com

Printed in U.S.A.

ABOUT THE AUTHOR

Charlotte Douglas has loved a good story since she learned to read at the age of three. After years of teaching that love of books to her students, she now enjoys creating stories of her own. Often her books are set in one of her three favorite places: Montana, where she and her husband spent their honeymoon; the mountains of North Carolina, where they're building a summer home; or Florida, near the Gulf of Mexico on Florida's west coast, where she's lived most of her life.

Books by Charlotte Douglas

HARLEQUIN AMERICAN ROMANCE

HARLEQUIN INTRIGUE

*Identity Swap

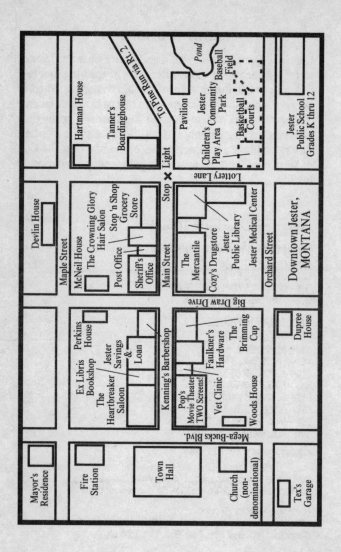

Prologue

"*Everything?*"

Jennifer Faulkner's knees buckled. Clutching her portable phone with a white-knuckled hand, she sank into the nearest chair in disbelief.

"Including Cottonwood Farm." The Montana attorney's Western twang resonated in her ear. "And your grandfather's recent lottery winnings. He left all he had to you."

"I see."

But Jennifer didn't see at all. For the last ten years, her grandfather had wanted nothing to do with her. He'd ordered her off the farm after her grandmother's death. Why had he made *her* the sole beneficiary of his estate?

"There would have been a hefty inheritance tax," the lawyer continued, "but your grandfather anticipated that and put the money in a trust for you, one worth over a million dollars."

"A million dollars," Jennifer murmured, while her mind reeled with shock.

She didn't want the money. She wanted Gramma Dolly and Grandpa Henry, alive. She longed for the warm cozy kitchen of Cottonwood Farm outside Jester in southeast Montana, where she'd spent all her holidays and vacations as a child while her jet-setting parents traveled the globe. But even a million dollars couldn't bring her beloved grandparents back.

"Ms. Faulkner? Are you still there?"

"Sorry. What were you saying?"

"It would help if you'd come out here and look over the farm. And I have papers for you to sign. My office is in Pine Run, the county seat, just southwest of Jester. Are you familiar with the town?"

"I was, ten years ago."

"Hasn't changed," the attorney said with a laugh. "My office is directly across from the entrance to the courthouse."

"And your name again, please?" In her shock, she'd forgotten it.

"Durham. Hank Durham."

She couldn't help smiling. In Montana, even lawyers had names like rodeo riders.

Montana.

Home.

"When can I expect you?" the lawyer asked.

She swallowed hard against her rising nostalgia. "I have to make some plans. I'll let you know."

Jennifer clicked off the phone and sank deeper into her chair. The day had certainly taken an unexpected turn. When she'd awakened this morning with wind-blown snow howling between the Chicago high-rises on the street where she lived, she'd known instantly she couldn't face another day as administrative assistant to Brad Harrison at Lake Investment Consultants. She'd called in sick, planning to use the day to write her resignation letter.

So Hank Durham's revelation couldn't have come at a better time. She was ready to move on and leave Chicago behind. She glanced around the tiny apartment with its rented furniture. Moving would be easy. Except for the terra-cotta saucer filled with fragrant paperwhites, the framed photograph of her grandparents on their fortieth wedding anniversary and the translucent, highly polished moss agate Luke McNeil had given her that special summer ten years ago, nothing else in the apartment besides her clothes belonged to her.

Luke McNeil.

The man had broken her heart and now his memory often stalked her waking hours and sometimes haunted her dreams, even after an entire decade without her laying eyes on him or hearing his voice. But what did she expect? How could she forget a man she'd loved for twenty-three years, ever since he'd saved her life when she was five years old?

Closing her eyes, she could see the high prairie that ran between the Faulkner and McNeil farms, could feel the warm summer breeze that had rippled the thick blue grama grass and sent yellow and pink wildflowers bobbing on that long-ago June afternoon, could smell the prairie coneflowers dancing in the wind.

"Race you to the creek," Vickie McNeil, Luke's younger sister had called. "Loser has to slop the hogs."

Jennifer loved the McNeil piglets, but she hated the big sows and shivered with fear whenever she was near them. Vickie's challenge put wings on her feet. Jennifer's sneakers pounded the packed-earth path that led to the creek and the footbridge. The sun baked her face, and the sound of Vickie gaining on her spurred her faster. Her momentum carried her onto the rustic log bridge where spray from the creek, swollen over its banks with snowmelt, slicked the surface. Before she could slow down, she found herself pitching headfirst into the swiftly moving stream.

She didn't know how to swim, and even if she had, she was no match for the raging current.

The last sound she heard before the freezing water closed over her head was Vickie's panicked scream.

Then, miraculously, strong hands grasped her arms and yanked her to the surface.

"Kinda cold for a swim, short stuff." Ten-year-old Luke's voice was teasing, but worry etched his face as he dragged her onto the bank next to his fishing pole and creel.

"I fell." She bit her lip, holding back tears. Luke McNeil was her hero, and she didn't want to embarrass herself further in front of him. Her good intentions, however, ended up on the creek bed, along with the creek water she'd swallowed. Mortified at throwing up, she sat shivering in her wet clothes.

"Hell, Jenny, your knee's bleeding like a stuck pig." Luke yanked a rag from his fishing creel, dipped it in the creek, then wrung out the excess water. He sponged the blood from her leg with the same gentleness she'd often seen him display with a newborn foal or a sick calf. "You must have banged it on a rock when you went under."

"I heard you, Luke McNeil. *Hell*'s a bad word, and Mama's gonna wash your mouth out with soap." Vickie stood beside him with her hands on her hips, outrage mixed with concern as she craned her neck, peering over Luke's shoulder to inspect Jennifer's injury.

"She won't know if you don't tell her. Besides, now you've said it, too."

Luke's face lit up in a slow grin, and Jenny's childish heart flip-flopped. His coal-black hair, straight and thick, his high cheekbones and his tanned skin indicated a Native American ancestor— probably Crow or Sioux—in his otherwise Scottish family tree. His only Celtic feature was his eyes, deep and blue as a Highland loch. Otherwise, with the exception of his jeans, boots and T-shirt, he could have been mistaken for a young brave. Jennifer had watched him run like the wind and ride as if he'd been born in the saddle, hence her hero worship. The strength he'd exhibited in pulling her from the powerful current had been extraordinary for a boy his age, another reason for admiration.

With a tenderness that won her heart, he cleaned her scrapes in the shade of the willows and cottonwoods, then tore a section off his shirttail and tied it around her knee as a bandage. His mother had later given him a tongue-lashing for ruining his newest shirt.

Jennifer had secretly washed the scrap of cloth and kept it in her box of special treasures until the year she left Cottonwood Farm for good, the same year Luke had asked her to marry him.

Yes, she'd fallen in love with Luke McNeil that morning twenty-three years ago, and in spite of a heap of trying, she hadn't been able to get him out of her mind or heart since. Luke was probably the reason things hadn't worked out with Brad Harrison. Or any other of the dozen men she'd dated before Brad. Who could compete with such a paragon?

As if conjured up by her thoughts, the phone rang and Brad was on the line.

''I need you here on the double, Jen. You know

the Radner-Whitcomb account by heart, and they're due any minute.''

''Call a temp. I'm not coming in.''

''Not at all today?''

''Not ever. You'll have my resignation on your desk in the morning.''

''But what'll I do? You're the only one who knows where everything is.''

''Everything,'' she said with immense satisfaction, ''is in my office. Help yourself.''

She clicked off the phone before he could protest, and experienced only the slightest twinge of conscience. She'd looked at Brad Harrison in a new light ever since that disastrous trip to Paris a few weeks ago. He had promised her a romantic vacation, just the two of them in the City of Lights. He'd neglected, however, to mention there would also be a consortium of French brokers and investors, meetings that ran from early morning to past midnight, and enough work for a secretarial staff of five— which Brad expected Jennifer to handle on her own.

Some romantic vacation.

Worst of all, when they returned to Chicago, Jennifer had a message waiting from Finn Hollis, her grandfather's friend. When she returned Finn's call, she'd learned that while she was slaving away in Paris, her grandfather had died, and she had missed his funeral.

Guilt racked her. She should have contacted her grandfather two months ago. For days, every time she had picked up a newspaper or turned on the television, she had seen pictures of Grandpa Henry and the others from Jester who'd pooled their money and won the Montana Big Draw. According to the reports on the "Main Street Millionaires," the participants had each put in a dollar a week for over eight years. Her grandpa's pal, Dean Kenning, the local barber, had driven to Pine Run every Monday morning to play twelve different tickets. When one of the tickets won, the participants had split forty million dollars twelve ways. Her grandfather's share, after taxes, was a little more than one million.

"Awesome." Brad knew she'd lived in Jester and had recognized her grandfather's name. "You should go visit the old guy. Tell him I'll give him good advice on investing his windfall."

Jennifer, who'd been contemplating contacting her grandfather before the publicity, changed her plans. "I can't call him now."

"Why not?" Brad asked.

She longed for Grandpa Henry and Cottonwood Farm with all her heart, but she'd left under awkward and unpleasant circumstances. Resuming their relationship after a ten-year hiatus had seemed unlikely before. Now it seemed downright impossible. "After all these years, he'll think I'm only after his money."

"You can convince him otherwise," Brad reasoned, but Jennifer hadn't been so sure.

She'd never understood why her grandfather had

asked her to leave in the first place. All he'd said was that he couldn't stand the sight of her. Not an auspicious basis for reestablishing a relationship.

For months after leaving the farm, Jennifer had written her grandfather and called repeatedly. Her letters had been returned and her calls had gone unanswered. Even three years ago when her parents died in a plane crash, and she'd discovered they'd squandered all their money on bad investments and high living, her grandfather hadn't called. She'd left more messages, but he hadn't responded. Fearful of another rejection, she hadn't called again. And now it was too late. Forever. Filled with grief and homesickness, Jennifer watched the blizzard rage outside her window.

Hank Durham had just provided her with the perfect excuse for returning to Jester. But with her grandfather dead and Luke McNeil only a memory, what was the point?

Chapter One

One week later

Sheriff Luke McNeil ran his fingers through his thick, black hair and scowled at the white stuff swirling outside the window of his office. March had come in like a lion. Looked like it would go out like a lion, too. How could he conduct a proper investigation of the collapse of the pavilion in the town park when its ruins were buried under four feet of ice and snow?

Without further evidence, he didn't know whether he had an accident, malicious mischief or even an attempted homicide on his hands, and not knowing made him edgy. His job was to protect the people of Jester, and he couldn't do that without knowing all the facts.

Thank God no one had been killed, although what Jack Hartman and Melinda Woods, the town vets, had been doing in the structure, no one knew.

Scratch that, he thought with a slow grin. He didn't have to be Sherlock Holmes to figure out the purpose of their secret meeting. Barely revived from her concussion and sporting bruised ribs from the pavilion's collapse, Melinda had laid her claim on Jack last night right outside Doc Perkins's clinic, with half the town as witnesses. Luke rubbed the back of his neck, remembering how Jack had watched in amazement when Melinda called Buck, a stray mutt no one else could tame, to heel. And just as docile as that wily dog, Jack had wrapped his arms around Melinda and asked her to marry him.

Luke's smile faded. But why had the blasted pavilion collapsed in the first place? And if it hadn't been an accident, were the vets the intended victims? If so, a motive eluded him. Although some farmers had balked at having a female veterinarian treat their animals, Luke hadn't picked up on anyone with enough animosity toward Melinda or Jack to wish them harm.

He shifted in his chair and propped his feet on his desk. If the damned snow would just stop long enough for the sun to come out and melt the accumulation atop the collapsed structure, he could inspect the wreckage, instead of sitting cooped up in his office, badgered by what-ifs.

Even if he hadn't heard the weather report, the evidence outside his window was overwhelming. The snow wasn't going to abate anytime soon. He might as well catch up on the paperwork stacked precariously on the corner of his desk, ready to slide into an avalanche if he didn't tackle it immediately.

He was reaching for the top folder when the door to the office opened and slammed against the wall. The same frigid blast that banged the door blew Wyla Thorne into the room.

An ill wind blows nobody good, Luke thought and suppressed a grimace.

He liked most folks just fine, but Wyla Thorne always set his teeth on edge. Maybe it was her knack for sticking her nose into other people's business that repulsed him. Or maybe it was how she flirted so shamelessly with him, despite the fact that she was over ten years his senior and had been through two nasty divorces.

She grabbed the door and struggled to shut it. Although she was about five foot eight inches tall, the woman didn't have an ounce of spare flesh on her, and even bundled up like an Eskimo, she appeared toothpick thin. Just as he was about to rise to help her, she managed to close the door against the bitter wind. When she turned back toward him, wisps of short red hair stuck out from the parka around her face, which displayed its usual pinched look, as if she'd just smelled or tasted something bad.

''You have to come quick, Sheriff,'' she stated breathlessly.

Luke ground his teeth. Her voice was a whine

worse than fingernails on a blackboard. He mentally added that to the list of things about Wyla that annoyed him.

"A problem?" In spite of his dislike, Luke was on his feet instantly and reaching for his coat.

"Amanda Bradley and Will Devlin."

"Again?"

Luke relaxed and sank back into his chair. Amanda and Dev had been fighting for at least two years over the building they owned jointly. Dev operated the Heartbreaker Saloon in his half of the structure, and Amanda ran the Ex-Libris Bookstore in hers. Oil and water. Just like their owners, the two businesses didn't mix. Dev was determined to buy out Amanda's half with his Big Draw winnings. Amanda was just as determined not to sell.

"They're at it worse than ever." Wyla nodded for emphasis and shed snow onto the office floor. "A real knock-down-drag-out."

"Come off it, Wyla. Their fights get pretty loud, but I've never known Dev and Amanda to exchange blows."

"They were close to it when I left them. Besides, if you don't break them up, they'll freeze to death."

Luke shook his head in disbelief. "They're outside? In this weather?"

"In their shirtsleeves."

He stifled a curse, tugged on his jacket and gloves, and reached for his hat. Seemed like his job more often required saving people from their own stupidity than it did protecting them from criminal elements.

Wyla scurried out the door ahead of him onto Main Street. Luke waded through the drifts to cross Big Draw Drive and headed past the barbershop toward the saloon. The wind practically blew Wyla ahead of him. She'd done her civic duty to alert him to trouble. Now she obviously intended to witness every juicy detail.

Other than Wyla, the street was deserted, as far as he could tell through the blowing snow. Folks in Jester had a healthy respect for the cold. Those who didn't, didn't survive. Dev and Amanda must have worked up a real head of steam to ignore temperatures lethal to a brass monkey. Luke could barely make out their arm-waving silhouettes on the sidewalk ahead, but the wind snatched their voices away from him.

He forced himself into a run. He had to get the idiots under cover before they both suffered frostbite and hypothermia.

Just as he came opposite the entrance to the bookstore, a customer, head tucked against the wind, arms filled with books, exited. Luke tried to slow his steps, but his boots hit a patch of ice.

In what seemed like slow motion but actually happened in seconds, Luke slid along the ice. Unable to stop, he slammed into the customer. The impact knocked them both off their feet and sent books flying. Fueled by a surge of adrenaline, Luke reacted instantly. If the woman was elderly, a fall on the ice could mean a broken hip, a potentially fatal injury. He had to break her fall. Wrapping his arms around her, he pulled her against his chest, cushioning the blow for her as he landed on his back.

He hit the sidewalk with such force it knocked the breath out of him, but not before he caught a whiff of roses, a familiar fragrance that filled him with nostalgia and overwhelming longing.

Stunned, he lay on the icy sidewalk with the woman atop him, every soft curve melded to him with an intimacy unimpeded by multiple layers of clothing. With her face buried in his neck, her breath warmed his skin, and he detected the lilting sound of her laughter above the howl of the wind and Wyla's screech of alarm.

Luke had barely drawn air into his lungs to ask if the woman was okay when she lifted her head. Her face hovered inches above his, and the sight knocked the wind out of him again.

Jennifer Faulkner!

Dark blond hair escaped from a knitted cap in seductive wisps that framed a face like an angel's. Laughter danced in her wide aquamarine eyes—an arresting shade of blue that had always reminded him of a tropical lagoon—and turned up the corners of her mouth into a kissable smile that showcased her delightful dimples. The cold had nipped her cheeks a delicious pink and reddened the tip of her small but perfectly formed nose, which had once sported an irresistible dusting of freckles.

When recognition suddenly lit her eyes, the laughter died in her throat and her smile faded. "Luke."

She scrambled quickly to her feet and would have fallen again if he hadn't pushed himself upright and caught her.

"Whoa, not so fast," he ordered, angry at himself for the longing that filled him, a longing he'd managed to bury for ten years. "Are you okay?"

She pulled her arm from his grasp, and he could have sworn the arctic temperature dropped another twenty degrees.

"I'm fine." Avoiding his gaze, she began gathering her books.

Dev and Amanda had apparently called a truce long enough to assist. Dev fished one of the books out of a snowdrift, but Amanda yanked it from him, wiped the snow off on the front of her cardigan and slipped it into the plastic bag she retrieved, which sported the distinctive Ex-Libris logo.

Jennifer hurriedly stuffed two more volumes into the bag, and Luke's keen investigator's eye couldn't help noticing the three titles: *Maximizing Your Real Estate Sale, Arizona Living* and *Investing for the Long Term.*

He wanted to confront her, to find out if the rumors he'd heard were true, but Amanda Bradley's shivers and the blue tinge to her lips reminded him of his mission.

"We're fine here, Amanda," he said. "You'd better get yourself inside where it's warm before you freeze to death."

"Freeze?" Dev said with a snort. "That woman's got a mad on that could scorch the whole town."

Luke turned on the bar owner with a glare that had stopped hardened felons in their tracks. "Anger only *seems* to protect you from the cold, and you're both prime candidates for frostbite and hypothermia. Now I suggest you each return to your own business before I have to arrest you for public disorderliness."

The bar owner opened his mouth as if to protest, but another look at Luke's expression apparently made him reconsider. He pivoted abruptly, an amazing maneuver on the icy sidewalk, and stalked back into the Heartbreaker Saloon without a backward glance.

With a sniff of disdain, Amanda spun on her heel and entered her bookstore, with Wyla Thorne right behind her, likely ready to pump Amanda for all the salient details of her latest battle with Dev.

Luke turned back to the sidewalk, prepared to confront Jennifer, and blinked in surprise.

She had disappeared.

For a moment, he drifted in a strange fugue state, similar to hundreds he'd experienced over the years after awakening from dreams of Jennifer—dreams that had seemed real. However, the ache where his backside had hit the sidewalk convinced him his latest encounter with the woman he'd loved so long ago hadn't been a dream this time. She'd been tantalizing flesh and blood, smelling of the same rose fragrance she'd used at eighteen, with her former American girl wholesomeness refined to a cool, elegant beauty by a decade of maturity. For a few brief moments, he'd held her in his arms again, and they ached now with the loss of her once more.

He gave himself a mental kick, disgusted that an infatuation from his youth still held a supposedly sensible thirty-three-year-old in its grip. Why was he surprised that Jennifer had disappeared? If she had any feelings at all, she should have been embarrassed to see him, especially since she owed him a heap of explaining about why she'd walked out on him without a fare-ye-well or by-your-leave ten years ago.

Although she'd exchanged Christmas and birthday cards and the occasional letter with his sister, Vickie, he had yet to hear doodley-squat from the woman who'd promised to marry him.

She'd disappeared then, too, just like today.

Like Dev and Amanda, Luke was now working up his own head of steam. Probably Jennifer had gone around the corner to his sister's house. Just as well. He didn't need to see her, to have all those old emotions stirred up again, to rub salt in old wounds. Best thing was to forget he'd seen her at all. Let her grab her granddaddy's money, sell his farm and hit the road again—apparently for Arizona this time, from the looks of her reading material—without shaking up the peaceful life he'd carved out for himself without her.

Who was he kidding?

Although he tried to attribute the ache inside him to the bitter cold, he'd experienced that same pain in the heat of summer. Why the hell did she have to show up now in Jester? Couldn't Henry's lawyer have taken care of the old man's estate and just mailed her a damned check?

He glanced up to find Amanda peering with a worried expression through the glass door of the bookstore. Wyla hovered behind her like an un-shakable shadow, taking in the sight of Jester's sheriff making a first-class fool of himself, standing in the dangerous cold like an idiot, pining over a lost love and risking the very frostbite he'd warned Amanda and Dev about.

After stamping his feet in an attempt to restore their circulation, he headed diagonally across Main Street and plowed through the drifts to the entrance of the Brimming Cup. Hot coffee and a bowl of Dan Bertram's famous chili should warm him up.

As Luke pushed through the front door and heard the familiar ring of the bell, the warmth of the large, airy diner enveloped him like a bear hug and an-other wave of nostalgia engulfed him.

The diner hadn't changed since Shelly Dupree's parents opened it in the fifties, except for an update of the country-and-western top ten songs available on the jukebox in the corner. The eatery looked just as it had when Luke had brought Jenny there for Mrs. Dupree's famous huckleberry pie after a Friday night at the movies. Like the street outside, the diner appeared deserted, except for the cook. There was no sign of Shelly or Valerie, the new waitress who had caused a stir weeks ago by abandoning her baby in Shelly's diner. Dan Bertram leaned with his arms crossed on the chrome-trimmed, gray Formica counter, scanning an edition of the *Pine Run Plain Talker*.

Wincing slightly, Luke slid his still-painful backside onto one of the high-backed chrome stools at the counter. At his arrival, Dan folded the paper, tucked it to one side and flashed a welcoming smile.

"You holding the fort?" Luke asked.

"All by my lonesome," the cook answered. "With this storm blowing, didn't figure we'd have much business. Suggested Shelly and Valerie stay home and keep warm. They took me up on it. What'll you have?"

"Coffee and a bowl of chili."

"Coming up."

While Dan filled his order, Luke glanced at the newspaper. It was an old issue, and the headline touted the upcoming Founders Day in Jester—held yesterday—reminding Luke of the mystery of the collapsing pavilion. He wrapped his mind around the intriguing problem, glad for anything that drove away thoughts of Jennifer Faulkner.

Dan returned with a thick white ceramic mug filled with steaming coffee and a bowl of chili, topped as Luke liked it with chopped onions and grated cheese.

Automatically, Luke picked up his food and carried it toward his usual spot, the rear booth, the last of six that lined the large picture windows overlooking the street. His thoughts still on the pavilion, he placed the bowl and mug on the table and swung onto the high-backed bench, upholstered in blue vinyl. He was halfway seated before realizing the other side of the booth was already occupied.

"Hello again, Luke. You following me?"

Double-dog damn. Jennifer.

Suspended half in the booth, half out, Luke considered his options. He could move to another table and look like a coward, or he could take his regular seat and prove to Jennifer she no longer affected him in any way.

How you gonna do that, cowboy? his conscience taunted him. *Stop breathing?*

With a sigh of resignation, Luke settled onto the bench. "Thought you'd headed for Vickie's."

"That's my next stop. I'm waiting for the storm to weaken."

"Might have a long wait. Don't you listen to the weather reports?"

She shook her head, and the delicate porcelain of her cheeks flushed. ''It's been too long. I'd forgotten how important weather is out here.''

''Seems like you've forgotten a lot of things.'' The words rushed out before he could stop them, and he cursed himself silently for giving her any hint that he might still care.

Avoiding his gaze, she glanced around the room. ''I haven't forgotten our—my favorite booth.'' She nodded toward his bowl. ''Or how good Dan's chili tastes. Or how his coffee's so strong you can stand a spoon in it. But it doesn't seem the same without Shelly waiting tables. I was hoping to see her.''

Jennifer had shed her hat, coat and gloves, and Luke couldn't help drinking in the sight of her. Instead of the sun-streaked blond ponytail he remembered, her hair had darkened, and she wore it in a sophisticated cut just above her shoulders that complemented the lift of her cheekbones and set off those magnificent aquamarine eyes.

Luke felt his old resentments start to soften at the sight, and he quickly hardened his heart. ''Too bad you couldn't get back to Jester just once to see your grandfather before he died. Must have broken his heart.''

The slash of crimson on her cheeks deepened. ''You'll never know how much I wanted to see him again.''

''Then why didn't you come?''

She dropped her gaze to her long, slender fingers

twined around the coffee mug in front of her. "Couldn't afford it," she murmured.

She was lying. In his business, Luke had learned to spot a liar a mile away. From the cut of her clothes, the styling of her hair, he could tell she hadn't sunk to the poverty level.

"Bus tickets are cheap," he said pointedly. "And Finn Hollis tells me you were in Europe when Henry died."

"That was business, paid for by the company I worked for."

"Convenient, wasn't it?" He couldn't hold back another dig. "Didn't have to spring the bucks to attend the funeral."

"I didn't know." The anguish in her voice was real. "I would have come, all the way from Europe, if I'd known."

The torment in her voice almost convinced him, until he remembered. "Yeah, most folks would travel halfway round the world to claim a million bucks."

Anger flashed in her eyes, creating a hurricane on that sea of tropical blue. "It wasn't like that. You don't understand."

A corresponding flash of temper rose within him. "Damn right I don't understand. Lots of folks in Jester don't understand. You want to clue me in?"

She thrust her chin in the air and met his eyes head-on. "I wanted to see Grandpa. I'd just about worked up the courage to make the trip when I saw the papers.''

''The Main Street Millionaires?''

She nodded glumly. ''I knew if I came back then, everyone, including Grandpa Henry, would think I'd come just for his money. I was still wrestling over what to do when I returned from Europe and heard Finn's message.'' The hurricane had vanished, leaving a calm sea of tears. ''It was too late for me to see Grandpa or attend his funeral.''

Forgotten emotions made Luke's usually reliable internal polygraph go haywire. Damned if he knew whether she was telling the truth or not, but he didn't trust her. She'd bamboozled him once. Big time. He wouldn't let it happen again.

''Too late for the funeral, but not too late for the money,'' he said, his voice heavy with sarcasm.

''I'd give it all away to have Grandpa back.'' A single tear slid from her eye and rolled down the curve of her cheek.

Luke resisted the urge to reach across the table and brush it away with his thumb. As sincere as she appeared, the facts spoke for themselves. She'd walked out on Henry—and Luke—ten years ago. She hadn't told Luke why, hadn't even said good-bye, and if she'd explained her leaving to Henry, he'd kept silent on the reason and taken it to his grave. In all those years, she hadn't contacted her grandfather or Luke.

Another unsolved mystery.

And if anything drove Luke wild, it was a puzzle that couldn't be explained.

Before he could question her further, Jennifer slipped from the booth and began tugging on her coat. Momentarily distracted by her long, slender legs, attractively encased in denim, he forgot everything but the look of her. Since she was about five foot eight, the top of her head had reached his jaw, and he remembered wrapping his arms around her and resting his chin on her hair. He could almost feel the heat of her arms around his waist, the pressure of her face against his chest—

"Sorry I didn't live up to your expectations." She had donned her hat and gloves and retrieved her bag of books. "Goodbye, Luke."

Before he could think of anything to say to keep her there—so he could ask more questions, he assured himself, not because he was enjoying her company—she exited the door in a flurry of snow and gusting wind.

He took a long sip of tepid coffee. Just as well. She would put the farm on the market, collect her money and be gone. With any luck, he'd never lay eyes on Jennifer Faulkner again.

Memory pulled him back ten years to this very booth, with the jukebox wailing in the corner and eighteen-year-old Jennifer, not across the table this time, but snuggled next to him on the seat, while they talked about their future together in Jester.

The next day, Jennifer's grandmother had died,

sending Jenny into grief and shock. She'd said hardly three words to him before or during the funeral. When he'd arrived at the farm the day after the Faulkners had buried Dolly, Henry had met him at the door.

"How's Jennifer?" Luke had asked, after expressing his condolences to Henry again.

"Gone."

At first, Luke feared grief had scrambled Henry's brain, so that the old man had confused his granddaughter with his wife.

"Jennifer's gone?"

"That's what I said. Took her to the bus station this morning. She should be in Billings now, catching a flight to Connecticut."

Luke had felt a momentary relief. "She's gone to her parents?"

Henry, his eyes wild with despair, his gray hair tousled, his clothes disheveled, had nodded. He obviously wasn't going to be forthcoming with any more information. Luke would have to pull it out of him.

"When will she be back?"

"Never."

Luke scrubbed a hand across his face, feeling as if he'd entered the twilight zone. Was Henry confusing Jenny with Dolly? Had the death of his wife of forty years made the old man lose his grip on reality?

"I meant when will Jennifer be back from Connecticut?"

Henry had fixed him with a piercing stare. "Let me say this once, son, and then don't ask me any more questions. Jennifer's never coming back to Jester. She's gone for good."

"Why?"

A tortured expression racked Henry's wrinkled face. "She didn't give me any explanation. Just said she'd never be back."

"What about me?"

"What about you?"

"Did she leave me a message, a note?"

"Sorry, son. She didn't mention you at all. Now leave me alone and let me mourn in peace."

Henry had shut the door in his face, and try as he might, for months after, Luke had never managed to extract any explanation for Jennifer's strange departure. She had never contacted him.

No phone calls.

No letters.

Nothing.

He'd tried contacting her at her parents' home, but they were somewhere in Europe and couldn't be reached, and Jennifer was apparently no longer in Connecticut. He'd done an Internet search for a phone anywhere in the country in her name, but the one Jennifer Faulkner he'd located had been seventy-eight years old and deaf as a post.

Devastated by Jennifer's desertion, he'd grieved

for weeks—until his anger had kicked in and saved him.

Jennifer Faulkner, in spite of her statements to the contrary, hadn't given a damn about Luke or being his wife. She'd played him for a fool....

Luke pulled his thoughts back to the present and shoved aside his untouched bowl of chili. His excursion into the past had killed his appetite. Jenny had disappeared ten years ago without an explanation. Now she had blown back into town, obviously unwilling to explain the past.

Or to stay.

Chapter Two

The arctic wind nipped Jennifer's cheeks, but she pushed ahead through the snow drifts along Big Draw Drive.

She should never have returned to Jester.

Luke was right. Folks didn't understand why she hadn't come back to visit her grandfather. And she couldn't explain. Without her grandfather to back up her story, they wouldn't believe it. Even after ten years, she could hardly believe it herself.

She'd wanted to see the farm and the town one last time, though. To place flowers on her grandparents' graves. To visit Vickie and meet her husband, Nathan, and their children. Jennifer had even hoped that running into Luke again might break the bond that had somehow remained forged between them all these years.

No such luck.

When she'd literally run into his arms outside the bookstore, she'd longed to hug him around the neck and hold on tight, feeling for the first time since her arrival that she'd really come home.

Not that Luke hadn't changed. If anything, he'd grown more handsome with age. But she'd sensed a brittleness and a deep sadness in him that she hadn't remembered. Maybe one of the dozens of women he'd dated, according to Vickie's letters, had broken his heart. If so, it served him right after the way he'd shattered hers, she told herself—even though deep down she couldn't stand the thought of Luke suffering.

Hard as she tried to hold on to that first glow of righteous indignation, she couldn't. With dismay, she recognized that her love for Luke ran so deep, she'd rather have him married to another woman, if that's what would make him happy, than to have him sad and lonely.

She reached the walk leading to the Perkins house and waded through the deep snow toward the front door, helped along by the wind gusting at her back.

Vickie must have been waiting for her, because the front door flew open as soon as Jennifer stepped onto the porch, and her old friend grabbed her and drew her inside. The warmth of the house and Vickie's welcoming hug enveloped her, driving away the cold and some of the pain from her meeting with Luke.

At least someone in town was glad to see her.

Vickie released her and stepped back. "Take off your coat and hat. Let me look at you."

Jennifer tugged off her cap, raked her fingers through her hair, shrugged out of her coat and handed her garments and book bag to Vickie, who placed them in the entry closet before pulling Jennifer into the cozy living room. With its creamy yellow walls, furniture upholstered in a muted yellow-and-blue plaid and bay window filled with lush green plants, the room appeared filled with sunshine, even though the storm raged outside.

"I should have known," Vickie said with an exaggerated frown, offset by the twinkle in her eyes. "You're as slender as you always were. Don't you ever gain a pound?"

"And you're as pretty as ever," Jennifer said, meaning every word.

Vickie's eyes were the same midnight-blue as her brother's, and her long, thick hair, tied back by a Hermes scarf, the same deep ebony as Luke's. About an inch shorter than Jennifer, Vickie had been trying to lose her "baby fat" as long as Jennifer could remember, but she carried the few extra pounds well, dressing with a sense of style that the girls in Jester had emulated during her high school days.

Judging from the flattering cut of Vickie's jeans, the sheen of her hand-tooled boots and the elegance of her burgundy twin set, Jennifer guessed her friend was still setting the fashion standards for the town.

"Motherhood agrees with you," Jennifer added.

"You'd think the little darlings would run these extra pounds off—" Vickie patted her hips for emphasis "—but no such luck."

Jennifer glanced around. "Where are they?" The only sign of children was the wicker chest overflowing with toys beside the fireplace.

"Taking a nap. With any luck, we'll have time for coffee and catching up on all the news before they wake up. Come on back to the kitchen."

Jennifer followed Vickie down a hallway into a kitchen with sunny-yellow walls, gleaming maple cabinets and French-blue countertops. "Your house is gorgeous. You really have an eye for decorating."

Vickie flashed her a grateful look. "Do you really like it? It's been fun fixing it up, but now I'll be starting all over again."

Vickie poured two mugs of coffee, waved Jennifer onto a high-backed maple bench in the breakfast nook, and settled across from her.

"Starting over?" Jennifer glanced at the showcase room. "But everything seems perfect as it is."

"Perfect, but too small. With three kids and only three bedrooms, we're cramped for space. Otherwise, I'd have invited you to stay here."

Jennifer smiled. "No problem. I'll enjoy the company at Gwen Tanner's boardinghouse."

Vickie's gaze scanned her face. Then, apparently satisfied that Jennifer was content with her arrangements, she continued. "Nathan's using part of our Big Draw winnings to build a new house."

"That's great. Congratulations, by the way. I saw you both on the news with the other Main Street Millionaires. I'm really happy for you."

"It's been fun," Vickie admitted. "I'm having a ball buying things for the kids, the new house and for myself." She touched the scarf that tied back her hair. Then her expression sobered. "I'm so sorry about your grandfather."

Jennifer nodded, unable to speak past the sudden knot in her throat.

"It's a shame you didn't get to see him before he died." Vickie's eyes held a question, the same one Luke had asked, but unlike her brother's censoring gaze, they held no condemnation.

Unable to explain, Jennifer changed the subject. "So where's this new house going to be?"

"Closer to Nathan's clinic and the school. On Lottery Lane."

Jennifer almost spat out her mouthful of coffee. "Lottery Lane?"

"Pretentious, isn't it?" Vickie said with a grimace. "Mayor Bobby Larson's got this wild hair up his behind. Wants to rename the town 'Millionaire.'"

"You're kidding!"

"Wish I were. He's also trying to talk the town council into building a big hotel where the park is."

"A hotel? What for? Nobody ever comes to Jester. Present company excluded."

"You should have been here a couple months ago. We were inundated with reporters and camera crews after the lottery drawing. Since then, Bobby's had this grandiose scheme of turning Jester into some kind of tourist attraction."

"What's to attract? Don't get me wrong. I loved it here. But unless things have changed, events in Jester are about as exciting as watching paint dry. Can't imagine the tourist buses pouring in for that."

"Nothing's changed—except for the lottery win. But that was enough to have Bobby renaming the streets and putting on airs. Calls himself Robert now."

Jennifer giggled. "That's quite a handle for a good-old-boy."

Sitting in the bright kitchen and gossiping with Vickie like old times eased the band of hurt Jennifer's encounter with Luke had tightened around her heart. Maybe, if she could just avoid him for the rest of her stay, coming back to Jester wouldn't have been a total mistake, after all.

"Have you seen Luke?" Vickie asked.

Jennifer composed her expression, unwilling to reveal how much that meeting had distressed her. "I literally ran into him outside the bookstore."

"And?"

"He was breaking up a fight between Will Devlin and Amanda Bradley." Jennifer pounced on the opportunity to change the subject again. "What's the problem with those two?"

Vickie clucked her tongue and shook her head. "It's a long story."

Jennifer nodded toward the snow blowing against the window. "I'm not going anywhere."

"Well, about eight years ago, Dev decided it was time for him to settle down, become respectable."

"Devil Devlin, the original bad boy?" Ten years older than Jennifer, Dev had been legendary for his wild and reckless youth. "Did they ever replace the screen at the cinema that he punctured with a bottle rocket?"

Vickie laughed. "They occasionally replace the duct tape they used to mend it. Anyway, Dev bought the Heartbreaker Saloon from his worthless uncle and has turned the place into a fairly respectable business, as saloons go."

"And Amanda?"

"She received the other half of the building in her mother's will. About two years ago, she opened Ex-Libris."

Jennifer nodded. "I never expected to find such a complete selection of books in Jester, of all places."

Vickie took a sip of her coffee. "Too bad Amanda doesn't have a larger clientele. If it weren't for Finn Hollis's recent addiction to collecting rare books, which he can now well afford with his lottery winnings, Amanda would have gone out of business long ago.''

"It's a great little shop, especially the comfy leather chairs in the sitting area.''

"And the ever-present teapot and pastries provided by Gwen Tanner. The kids and I love it,'' Vickie said, "but it doesn't have much appeal to cowboys and farmers. Most of them are too busy earning a living to have time to read.''

"And when they do find time,'' Jennifer added, "I suppose they spend it at the saloon. Is that the sore spot between Amanda and Dev?''

"In a roundabout way. Dev's business is good, and he wants to expand. He's tried to buy Amanda out with his lottery money, but she won't budge. She's determined to make her bookstore a success. And she claims the riffraff who frequent his bar are driving her customers away.''

Jennifer got the picture. "Amanda had a Mozart CD playing while I was there, but I could barely hear it over the noise coming from next door. 'If I hear that jukebox blasting through the wall one more time,' Amanda said, 'I'll go stark raving mad.' She asked Irene Caldwell to wait on me. Then she marched out onto the street without even stopping for a coat. The next thing I knew, I could hear Dev and Amanda having at it, even over the wail of the country-and-western song from the bar.''

"And that's when Luke showed up?" Vickie asked.

"Apparently alerted by Wyla Thorne."

Vickie frowned. "That busybody. Her nose has been out of joint ever since she declined to play the lottery the week they won."

Jennifer could feel the tension draining out of her in the warmth of the kitchen and the glow of Vickie's friendship. She'd successfully avoided talking about Luke, and was enjoying the town gossip. She felt almost as if she'd never left Jester.

"So—" Vickie leaned forward and skewered her with a glance "—did you talk to Luke?"

Jennifer squirmed. She should have known her friend wouldn't let her off that easily. "Briefly. He didn't seem particularly glad to see me."

Vickie reached over and covered Jennifer's hand with her own. "What happened between you two? Ten years ago, I'd have bet the farm that you'd be together for the long haul."

Jennifer took a deep breath to stop the tears that threatened to well up in her eyes. "You'll have to ask Luke."

Vickie knitted her eyebrows. "He won't talk about you."

"Guess he's too busy playing the field, like you said in your letters." Jennifer leaned back and crossed her arms over her chest, wishing for a way to change the topic. Talking about Luke hurt. Thinking about Luke hurt. And she feared that be-

ing so close to him again after so many years was
going to hurt even more.

"He dates a lot," Vickie admitted. "You remember how women were around him? Well, his
appeal hasn't changed. But none of them make him
happy. Not like you did."

If I made him so happy, why didn't he ever con-
tact me?

"That was a long time ago," Jennifer said with
all the casualness she could muster. "People
change."

"Well, Luke certainly has."

"How?" The question erupted before Jennifer
could remind herself that she'd wanted to talk about
something or someone else.

Vickie shrugged. "He's harder, somehow. Takes
everything so seriously. Something—" she cocked
an eyebrow and considered Jennifer "—or somebody has wounded him deeply."

Jennifer held up her hands and struggled to keep
her voice light, without bitterness. "Don't look at
me. I haven't been here. Must have been one of his
bevy of beauties."

"Maybe," Vickie said thoughtfully. "Anyway,
the only time he's his old self is when he plays
with the kids. You know he's always wanted a
houseful of his own."

Jennifer's heart lurched with pain. She and Luke
had talked about children—how much they were

looking forward to having them, how many they wanted, what names they would give them.

A sleepy face poking around the hall door saved her from more heartbreaking thoughts. ''Speaking of kids—''

Vickie turned toward the door. ''Hey, baby. Come meet your aunt Jennifer.''

''Hi, Caitlyn,'' Jennifer said softly. ''You're a sweetheart.''

The toddler, clutching a well-worn teddy bear by its arm, streaked toward her mother and buried her face in her lap, then turned and peered toward Jennifer with one big brown eye.

''Caitlyn's shy,'' Vickie explained.

''Brown eyes, blond hair,'' Jennifer observed. ''Must get her looks from Nathan.''

''They all do,'' Vickie said without a hint of regret, ''and I couldn't be more pleased.''

''You're a lucky woman.''

A strange expression flitted across Vickie's face. ''I really am. So much so, it scares me.''

''What do you mean?''

''I have Nathan, three wonderful children, and now we've won the lottery. I'm afraid I'm tempting fate.''

''Nonsense,'' Jennifer insisted. ''I like to believe that good things come to good people.''

Vickie laughed. ''Then something extraordinary is coming to you, Jennifer, because as far as people are concerned, I've always considered you one of the best. I'm so glad you're back in Jester.''

''But only for a short while.''

Vickie's face fell. ''You're not staying?''

Jennifer shook her head. ''Never planned to. I came to meet with Hank Durham, Grandpa's lawyer. Then I'll list the farm with a real estate agent and I'm outta here.''

Vickie cocked an eyebrow again and the corners of her perky mouth lifted with interest. ''You have somebody waiting for you back in Chicago?''

With distaste Jennifer remembered Brad Harrison and what a loser he'd been. ''I'm not going back to Chicago.''

Picking up Caitlyn, who settled into her lap with her eyelids drooping, Vicki considered Jennifer over her daughter's silky curls. ''Moving again? When we were kids, you always talked about putting down roots in Jester.''

''It's great being here with you, Vickie, but—'' Jennifer shrugged ''—with my grandparents gone…''

Vickie sighed. ''Where to this time?''

''I'm leaning toward somewhere warm. Maybe Arizona. Or even Florida.''

Jennifer didn't know why she'd chosen those states. The milder climate had its charm, but she really didn't mind the cold. She had a bundle of fond memories of Christmases and spring breaks at Cottonwood Farm, snowbound with her grandparents, when Vickie and Luke had hooked up the McNeil horses to a sled and braved the elements for a visit.

"You're a little young to retire," Vickie said, "although since you've inherited Henry's winnings, I suppose you can if you want."

Jennifer searched for words to give voice to the restlessness and dissatisfaction she felt, but she couldn't find them, as much as she longed to share her feelings with her friend. She was looking for something, but she didn't know what. Or didn't want to admit, even to herself, that she was longing for a love like she'd once shared with Luke. She feared, however, that that love had been a once-in-a-lifetime experience, one she wouldn't be lucky enough to encounter again.

At least, she consoled herself, she wouldn't have her heart broken again, either.

Weariness seeped through her, and she stifled a yawn.

Across the table, Vickie knotted her brows. "You look bushed. Did you sleep last night?"

"I drove straight through. Wanted to beat the storm here this morning. And wanted to get here before my car conked out completely. It started making funny noises outside of Fargo."

"Tell you what. Why don't you go back to the boardinghouse and get some sleep? Come back here for supper at seven. Nathan will be home then, and you can meet Ricky and Shannon when you're rested. They'll wear you out otherwise.''

Jennifer hesitated, but the prospect of spending the evening by herself in her very comfortable but lonely room at Gwen Tanner's helped her make up her mind. ''I'd love to come. But don't go to any trouble for me.''

''No trouble. As far as I'm concerned, you're one of the family.''

The sincerity in her friend's voice was a pleasant contrast to Jennifer's chilly encounter with Luke. ''I'll be here at seven.''

Vickie stood, scooping up Caitlyn in her arms, and with her daughter dozing on her shoulder, walked Jennifer to the door.

A few minutes later, head bent into the wind as she struggled along snow-clogged Main Street toward the boardinghouse, Jennifer wondered if the glint she'd noted in Vickie's eyes when she said goodbye was a trick of the light or a sign of the mischief for which her friend was famous.

Must have been the light, Jennifer decided, unable to think what trick a grown-up Vickie with three children might play on her childhood friend.

LUKE ENTERED HIS OFFICE and resisted the urge to lock the door behind him. Surely Wyla wouldn't follow him again.

He'd barely managed to escape her in the diner, where she'd appeared as soon as Jennifer had left, asking oblique questions in an attempt to pump him for particulars on his run-in with Jennifer. He'd pretended not to hear, but with the persistence of a terrier after a rat, she'd asked again.

"Sorry, Wyla," he'd said, "but I can't stop to chat now. I was up all night cordoning off the pavilion before the storm arrived, and I have a mountain of paperwork on my desk. Have to get back to work."

His excuse had been truthful. The inside of his eyelids felt like sandpaper, his mind was fuzzy from lack of sleep and the files on his desk reproached him. For a moment he thought longingly of the cot in the lockup in the back room. With the snow and wind raging outside, Jester was unlikely to experience a crime spree before the weather calmed, but he knew if he lay down, he'd be plagued by memories of Jennifer Faulkner—and the reality of the beautiful woman she'd become.

Resigned to his clerical tasks, he refilled the coffeemaker with water and fresh grounds and flipped the switch. Settling into his desk chair, he grabbed the folder he'd abandoned when Wyla had blown into the room earlier. But he couldn't concentrate on the report of the arrest of a drunk and disorderly patron at the Heartbreaker Saloon night before last.

His eyes kept straying to the calendar on the wall beside him.

It was ten years ago this month that he'd first realized he loved Jennifer Faulkner. That fact had hit him out of the blue, like a lightning bolt on a clear morning. The winter had been mild that year and mid-March unusually warm, thanks to El Niño—or was it La Niña? Luke could never keep the genders of those weather systems straight. At any rate, he'd had the day off from his job as a Pine Run deputy and had agreed to Vickie's request to drop her off at Cottonwood Farm. Jennifer had arrived from the expensive boarding school she attended in New England, to spend spring break with her grandparents.

Dolly Faulkner had met them at the door with a hug for each and the mouthwatering aroma of cinnamon buns wafting from the hallway behind her. "Come into the kitchen. Coffee's on and the rolls are hot."

Dolly was like a second mother, hard to say no to. Besides, Luke had no plans for the day, his stomach was growling with hunger, especially after a whiff of Dolly's specialty, and he always enjoyed the Faulkners' lively company.

He'd followed Vickie and Dolly into the kitchen, where Henry had sat at the round oak table, smooth and shiny as glass from Dolly's constant scrubbing, and smelling pleasantly of lemon oil. Everything in the room glistened and sparkled under Dolly's care.

Even Henry.

Luke couldn't remember ever seeing Henry when he didn't look as if he'd been scrubbed and dressed for Sunday school. When the old man had owned his hardware store on Main Street, he'd come to work each day in a fresh chambray shirt, starched so stiff it rattled, and jeans or slacks with a crease sharp enough to cut butter. His gray hair, thinning at the crown, was cropped close. Henry had once attempted to grow it long enough for a comb-over to disguise his balding scalp, but Dolly wouldn't have it. Said it made him look like an old man. Luke had heard she'd made a pact with Dean Kenning, the barber, so that no matter what Henry requested when he went into Dean's shop for a clip, he always received the same close cut.

Remembering, Luke smiled. Dolly and Henry had been an unlikely match. She was bubbly and talkative, with a personality like summer sunshine. Henry was taciturn, withdrawn, and seemed to live under a thundercloud, but the love between them was so palpable you could almost feel it when they were together.

Their appearances were as opposite as their natures. Dolly was short and plump, barely chest-high to her gaunt, long-legged husband. Jennifer had apparently inherited the best of each of her grandparents. Except for being tall and long-legged like her grandfather, she looked exactly like Dolly with her dark blond hair, aquamarine eyes and pretty face that lit up like a summer day when she smiled. The only other trait of Henry's she'd inherited was a touch of his aloof nature, which manifested itself in Jennifer as shyness.

Henry had glanced up with what passed for a smile when Vickie and Luke came into the kitchen. "Hello there, McNeil young'uns. Jennifer will be down in a minute. Have a seat."

Luke sat next to Henry, facing the door to the hall. Vickie sat across from him, and Dolly set a plate with a cinnamon bun the size of a saucer in front of each of them, then turned back to the stove for the enamel pot that always held simmering coffee.

"How're things over in Pine Run?" Henry asked. "Any crime sprees we should know about?"

Luke grinned. In Pine Run, three parking tickets and a jaywalker counted as a crime wave. "Things are quiet. Folks getting ready for spring. You putting in a crop this year, Henry?"

Henry nodded. "Sugar beets."

Dolly appeared at Luke's elbow with a cup of coffee for him. "Tell me, Luke, how come a handsome young man like you isn't married yet?"

Luke took a sip of Dolly's famous brew and rose to the bait. It was a game they'd played ever since Luke had graduated from high school five years earlier. "You know the answer to that, Mrs. Faulkner. I'm waiting for Jenny to grow up so I can marry her."

At that moment he glanced at the doorway, saw Jennifer standing there, and felt his heart stop in his chest. As if blinders had fallen from his eyes, he realized that Jenny was no longer the gawky, skinny little kid who'd played with his sister and followed him around like a puppy. The beautiful woman she'd become made his mouth go dry. Her designer jeans, obviously bought in some back-East boutique, definitely not at the Mercantile in Jester, hugged hips with just the right amount of curve to drive a man wild, and sheathed legs that seemed to go on forever. A tooled belt with a silver buckle cinched her tiny waist, and the crisp, white shirt, open at the neck, revealed a delectable hint of cleavage.

As seductive as her body had become, her face was even more alluring. Gone were the awkward planes of childhood, even though a sprinkle of freckles still graced the bridge of her nose. Her high cheekbones, small but regal nose and tilted chin would put Madison Avenue's highest-paid model to shame. Long, dark lashes framed eyes the most startling shade of blue, and her sun-streaked blond hair was caught up in a sophisticated French braid with enchanting wisps of curls framing her remarkable face.

Pretty little Jenny Faulkner had grown into a woman. The woman, Luke realized with a jolt, that he'd been waiting for all his life.

His retort to Dolly was no longer a joke, but God's own truth. He'd been waiting for Jenny to grow up so he could marry her.

Chapter Three

Luke shoved back from his desk, trying to push away the memories as well, without success. That morning ten years ago, he'd fallen in love with the woman that little Jenny Faulkner had become.

And it hadn't been just her sudden physical maturity that had hooked him. He'd always found Jenny's personality appealing, from the streak of mischief that kept him looking over his shoulder and watching his step whenever he knew she was around, to the deep affection and devotion she displayed toward her grandparents, and the sense of humor that erupted unexpectedly, like sunshine from behind the cloud of her shyness.

He couldn't shake the recollection of that distant March morning. "I'm waiting for Jenny to grow up so I can marry her," he'd said.

She'd tossed him a challenging glance as she took her seat at the table. "That dog won't hunt, Luke McNeil. I turned eighteen in January. You'll

have to find another excuse besides me for not settling down.''

"Luke's still sowing his wild oats," Vickie
teased, "and wild barley, wild rye, wild corn—"

"Best not to aggravate your brother when he's
wearing a gun," Luke warned with a twinkle in his
eyes.

"But you're off-duty," Jennifer said, her eyes
searching Luke for signs of a weapon.

"It's in a holster at the small of my back," he
explained, "under my sweater. And no need to
worry. I took an oath never to shoot my kid sister,
no matter how big a pain in the a—er, neck she
becomes.''

Vickie flashed her brother a grin and wiped icing
from the corner of her mouth with her little finger.

"Besides," Luke continued, unable to take his
eyes off Jennifer, "I've had enough of the single
life. It's time I did settle down.''

Vickie's mouth dropped open in surprise. "You
feeling okay?''

"Best I've felt in years.''

Luke winked at Jennifer across the table and was
rewarded with a delightful blush that spread from
the open V of her blouse to the curves of her
cheeks. Vickie and Henry seemed oblivious to the
exchange, but Dolly glanced from Luke to Jennifer
with a knowing smile, like the cat that ate the
cream.

"So what are your plans after graduation?" Luke

asked Jennifer, suddenly hungry to learn all he could about her. "Going to college?"

Jenny shook her head. "I'll be coming here as soon as school's out. Figured I'd take a year off to decide what I want to do."

"Maybe you could find a job, like I did," Vickie suggested. A year older than Jennifer, she'd gone to work recently as a receptionist at the new clinic in town opened by Dr. Nathan Perkins.

"I'll have plenty to do here at the farm," Jennifer said, "helping Gramma and Grandpa."

Dolly reached over and gave her granddaughter's hand a squeeze. "We're looking forward to having you, child. And I'll certainly enjoy the company. Gets lonesome here at times."

Even though Henry had sold his hardware business, he apparently missed downtown life, Luke thought. Between morning and evening chores, Henry spent most of his time at the barbershop, jawing with Dean Kenning and Finn Hollis, his two best buddies. Luke expected Dolly did find the farm lonely for most of the day.

"So." Dolly shook off her momentary melancholy. "What are you young people up to today?"

Jennifer glanced at Vickie with raised eyebrows. "How about a movie?"

"Sounds good to me," Vickie replied, "if Luke will drive us into town."

"Take my truck." Luke tossed the keys to

Vickie, who fumbled them in her amazement at the offer. "I'll walk home."

"You're welcome to come with us," Jennifer said, her offer a blend of shyness tinged with anticipation.

Lord knew, he'd wanted to go, but he'd had to talk to Henry first. "Thanks. Maybe next time."

The girls left, and while Dolly cleared the table, Luke followed Henry to the barn. He had tremendous respect and affection for the old man, and he wasn't about to ask Jennifer for a date without her grandfather's approval.

Luke's request had caught Henry by surprise. He'd run his fingers over his close-cropped hair and shook his head. "I still think of Jenny as if she's ten years old."

"She grew up while we weren't looking."

"You're a good bit older than she is. Five years or so, isn't it?" The lines in Henry's face deepened with a frown.

"Old enough to treat her with more respect than some randy teenager might," Luke countered.

The old man had agreed, but cautioned him that Jenny was a good girl, and he didn't want her reputation spoiled by any "monkey business," Henry's euphemism for sex.

"Anything like that goes on," Henry had warned, "and I'll come after you with the Winchester I keep over the fireplace for vermin."

Luke had promised Henry, and it turned out to

be the hardest promise he'd ever had to keep, because he'd never wanted any woman, before or since, as much as he'd wanted Jennifer. And what he'd felt had been more than physical attraction. He'd loved her with a passion that had alarmed him with its intensity.

And he'd believed she'd loved him the same way.

What a fool he'd been.

A flurry of motion drew his attention to the window. Jennifer, chin tucked against the wind, was struggling along Main Street. At the sight, a disturbing combination of desire and anger blossomed within him. He wondered if she was headed for her car, and for an instant worried about her driving in the vicious storm.

Then he reminded himself that Jennifer's welfare wasn't his business, hadn't been his business for over ten years. Hell, her welfare had probably *never* been his business. He'd been just too damned gullible not to recognize it.

As much as he tried to hold that hardened attitude, his heart told him differently. He remembered the tears in Jenny's eyes the night he'd asked her to marry him. They'd been tears of joy and happiness, something pretty tough to fake. And there'd been nothing false about her kisses, either. Recalling her lips against his, the curves of her body contoured against him, the sweetness of her breath, the tightening of her arms around his neck and the love radiating from her face when she gazed at him made him admit she'd cared for him.

Then what the hell had happened?

Should her reluctance to announce their engagement have been a clue? Luke hadn't thought so at the time. Jenny had worried that folks would think her too young for marriage, just months out of high school, so she'd asked Luke to wait until Christmas before they broke the news to anyone. She'd made him promise not to tell her grandparents, not even Vickie. At that point, she could have asked for the moon and he'd have given it to her. As it was, he'd planned to buy her the biggest diamond he could afford for a Christmas present.

At least the lack of an announcement had spared him public humiliation when she'd dumped him and returned East, but it hadn't saved him from a broken heart—and an anger that still festered to this day.

Poor old Henry. He'd never known how close Luke had come to marrying his granddaughter.

Luke slumped in his chair and stared across the desk at the seat Henry had occupied countless times before his death. On days when the barbershop had filled, demanding Dean's attention, and Finn had headed home with a new book for his collection under his arm, Henry had wandered into the sheriff's office in search of company.

The change in the old man after his wife's death and his granddaughter's desertion had been radical.

His formerly immaculate clothes had turned thread-bare and sported food stains and dirt. His close-cropped haircut, no longer mandated by Dolly, had turned into a shaggy mane. But worst of all had been the pain and sadness in the old man's eyes.

Something else had lingered there, too, something strangely resembling guilt, although Luke, for the life of him, had never been able to figure out what Henry Faulkner had to feel guilty about.

"You need to find yourself a good woman and settle down," Henry had advised him on more occasions than Luke could count. The old man never knew that Luke had once planned on marrying Jennifer and presenting him with great-grandchildren.

"And once you find that woman," Henry had said with a strange hitch in his voice, "don't ever take her for granted. Let her know every day how much you love her."

Remembering, Luke rubbed his weary eyes with his fists. He'd found that woman ten years ago, but things hadn't worked out, and to this day, he hadn't a clue why.

Another damned mystery he couldn't solve, he muttered to himself as he watched Jennifer disappear in a swirl of snow.

FOR THE UMPTEENTH TIME, Jennifer closed her eyes and tried to sleep, but her efforts at an afternoon nap proved futile. Not that the bed in the corner second-floor room of Gwen Tanner's boardinghouse wasn't comfortable. With its firm mattress, sheets that smelled of lavender and sunshine, and fluffy down comforter, it was a vast improvement over the rented bed she'd slept on in Chicago for the past year. Her inability to rest had nothing to do with furniture and everything to do with what was going on in her head.

And her heart.

If she'd known seeing Luke McNeil again would affect her so strongly, she would never have returned to Jester, she swore to herself. But she knew that she lied.

If she searched her soul, she'd have to admit that her desire to see Luke had been the motivating factor behind her visit to Montana. She'd hoped to lay his ghost to rest, prayed that meeting him in the flesh after all these years would verify her love for him as merely a teenage crush that she could then forget, making her free to love again.

Wrong.

If anything, seeing Luke again had rekindled the embers into flames, ones she seemed helpless to extinguish. Jennifer rolled onto her stomach and tugged a pillow over her head. If her car engine wasn't acting weird, she'd load her luggage as soon as the storm ended, sign Hank Durham's papers in Pine Run and keep heading south, all the way to Arizona.

Heading south.

She grimaced at the ironic phrase. That was the

direction her life had taken ever since she first left Jester.

She flipped onto her back with a sigh. She could run, but she couldn't hide. Her love for Luke hadn't been a girlish fling. It had been the real thing, lying dormant all these years, waiting to blossom back to life. Only problem was, Luke McNeil couldn't seem to stand the sight of her.

Sucking in a deep breath, she rolled off the bed and faced herself in the mirror over the bureau. She no longer had Luke's love, but she certainly had her pride. If she turned tail and ran after her first meeting with him, folks in Jester would put two and two together and come up with twenty. She had no desire to make her personal life fodder for town gossip by acting like an idiot. No, she'd have to tough it out, if only so she could face herself in the mirror without feeling like a coward.

After sluicing her face with water in the adjoining bathroom, she dragged a brush through her hair, added a touch of gloss to her lips and surveyed her clothes. Jeans, fisherman's sweater and boots would do for dinner at Vickie's, and especially for the trek through the snow to get there. A glance at her watch revealed the time was five o'clock, giving her almost two hours to kill before she was due at the Perkinses.

When Jennifer had returned to the boardinghouse from Vickie's earlier, she'd gone straight to the kitchen to inform Gwen she wouldn't be having supper with the other boarders. She'd found her hostess busy with meal preparations in the spacious room of the big Victorian house.

"Coming in here is like stepping back in time," Jennifer had said, smiling at her old friend.

During her vacations in Jester, she and Vickie had often visited with Gwen, who was Vickie's age, and Gwen's grandmother in this big, sunny kitchen, where the girls were usually treated to some delicacy, fresh and hot from the oven. Lacy molasses cookies, fragrant gingerbread, sticky buns or chewy brownies heavy with walnuts had been heaped on their plates, and frosty glasses of lemonade provided to wash them down. With its high ceilings, old-fashioned cabinets and farmhouse sink, the room brought back memories of long summer afternoons and culinary delights. It also stirred a poignant homesickness for her own grandmother that made Jennifer's heart ache.

At her voice, Gwen glanced up from the ramekins in which she was assembling what appeared to be chicken pot pies. Flour from a nearby pastry board dusted a strand of her dark auburn hair, and her green eyes flashed a cheerful hello before she bent again to her task.

"I've tried to keep the room like Grandmother had it," Gwen said, "but after the lottery, I decided to use some of my money to modernize."

"The improvements blend in well," Jennifer observed. "New six-burner cooktop, double oven, refrigerator in brushed stainless steel…and the old linoleum's gone.''

"Pergo," Gwen said with a nod toward the floor. "Great stuff, especially when there's a mess to clean up. Is there something you need?"

Jennifer shook her head. "My room's perfect."

"Good. I aim to please."

"Just wanted you to know I won't be here for supper. Vickie's invited me over at seven for a meal and to meet Nathan and the kids."

Gwen swiped at a stray lock of hair with the back of her hand. "You'll love Nathan. He's a great doctor. If you're ill, he makes you feel better just by being in the same room with him. And he's a wonderful family man, as dependable as the rising sun. And the kids are adorable. You'll want to steal them and take them home."

"Wherever that is," Jennifer murmured to herself.

Gwen squinted, eyeing her closely. "You feeling okay?"

Wondering if her heartache over Luke was visible, Jennifer resisted the urge to squirm. "Just tired after driving all night. I'm going up now to nap until it's time to head over to Vickie's."

"We're on an early schedule tonight. If the storm clears, Oggie Lewis has a meeting of the executive council of the PTA at the school."

"Mr. Lewis, the vice principal? I didn't know he lived here."

Gwen nodded. "He's a sweetheart. Treats me like his daughter, since he has no family of his own. We'll gather in the dining room for a glass of wine at five. Dinner's at five-thirty. Join us if you're awake by then. Have some wine or a cup of coffee. We're a lively group."

"Thanks." Jennifer started to leave, then turned back. "Gwen?"

"Yes?"

"It's good to see you again."

"You, too, Jenny. It's been too long."

Remembering their conversation later, Jennifer felt the warmth of friendship. Gwen Tanner hadn't asked questions or berated her for not coming back while her grandfather was alive. She'd given Jennifer a warm, unconditional welcome to the boardinghouse and made her feel like one of the family. Joining the others for a before-dinner drink suddenly seemed like a good idea.

Jennifer left her room and descended the staircase with its highly polished banister. A slightly built man in his late fifties, with salt-and-pepper hair, met her in the entry hall. "You must be Jennifer."

"And you're Mr. Lewis."

Although she'd never attended the school where he was vice principal, Jennifer recalled seeing the man around town. Her friends in Jester had always regarded him with a mixture of affection and respect. Today, instead of the business suit he'd usually worn, he was dressed in slacks, a crisp white shirt and tie, and a faded navy-blue cardigan with suede patches on the elbows.

"Call me Oggie," he said with a gentle smile, "otherwise the ladies here will think I'm being snooty. Stella's already in the dining room. Will you join us?"

With old-fashioned gallantry, he offered his arm, and Jennifer tucked her hand beneath his elbow. "I won't be having dinner—"

"You're dining at the Perkinses."

She suppressed a smile. Apparently Tanner's Boardinghouse had its own set of jungle drums where news traveled fast.

The front door rattled, and Irene Caldwell entered, buffeted by the wind. Benny, her Welsh Corgi, who'd apparently been watching from a parlor window, bounded in with all the energy of a puppy in spite of his twelve years, yapping happily at his owner's return. Irene scooped him up in her arms and hugged him, then set him at her feet.

"Don't know why Amanda insisted on keeping the bookstore open," the older woman said as she shed her coat and muffler. "Seldom has any business, even in good weather."

"Give her time," Oggie said consolingly. "It takes a while to build up a clientele. Meanwhile, it's good of you to help her out occasionally."

"Mostly I just keep her company. And it keeps me out of trouble," Irene said with a mischievous grin, stripping off her gloves and rubbing her hands together. "A glass of wine will hit the spot this afternoon. Get my blood circulating again. My feet are frozen."

The trio headed into the dining room, with Benny trotting at Irene's heels.

"Did you get back all right with your books?" Irene asked Jennifer. "That was quite a run-in you had with the law, if you'll excuse the pun."

Luke's scowling image flashed into Jennifer's mind. She forced the disturbing picture away. "The books are fine. Amanda wiped the snow off them, and I'm looking forward to reading them later tonight. I appreciate your help in selecting them."

Irene and Oggie moved into the dining room, but Jennifer paused on the threshold in admiration.

A huge mahogany dining table with a matching sideboard and china cabinet filled with classic Blue Willow dishes dominated the space, whose walls, like the rest of the house, were painted a soothing eggshell tint. A colorful Oriental rug in muted colors covered the gleaming hardwood floors, and a brass chandelier, probably the original gaslights converted to electricity, hung centered over the table, giving the room a cheerful glow in the early evening gloom.

A petite and slightly pudgy platinum blonde, dressed in a long denim skirt, white turtleneck sweater and fringed leather vest, stood at the sideboard, wine decanter in hand.

"I'm bartender tonight," she announced with a bubbly voice and a pleasing expression.

"Stella Montgomery," Oggie said, "let me introduce—"

"Don't be so stodgy, Oggie," Stella said with a friendly look and a softness in her voice that contradicted the reprimand. "Of course I know who this is. I remember Jennifer when she was knee-high to a grasshopper."

"Good to see you again, Miss Montgomery," Jennifer said.

"It's Stella, child. We aren't formal around here. Now, who wants a tipple?" She turned back to the sideboard, filled long-stemmed glasses with white wine and passed one to each boarder.

Gwen pushed her way through the swinging door from the kitchen, bearing a large tray from which emanated a mouthwatering aroma.

"Oh, my." Oggie licked his lips and placed his free hand over his heart like a lovesick boy. "Are those what I think they are?"

Gwen nodded. "Your favorite. Mushrooms and onions in puff pastry. Why don't you all have a seat? You can think of this as a first course."

Jennifer held back until the others had taken what she assumed were their regular places, then slipped into an empty chair. Although the sky had darkened outside and frost rimmed the windows, the dining room was snug and bright, reminding Jennifer of Gramma Dolly's kitchen on a winter's day. Slowly the pleasant atmosphere and crisp wine relaxed some of the tension still knotted inside her from her encounter with Luke.

Gwen handed the tray of hors d'oeuvres to Stella, but declined a glass of wine. After returning to the kitchen to retrieve a cup of tea, she sat at the head of the table.

Irene took the tray, inhaled with gusto and a longing look, but passed the delicacies immediately to Jennifer. "None for me. I love them, but they give me nightmares. My digestion isn't what it used to be."

Curled at her feet, Benny woofed with disappointment.

"Don't worry, boy," Irene assured the dog, "you'll get a taste. In spite of my protestations to the contrary, everyone in the house slips you tidbits under the table."

"Try some," Gwen encouraged Jennifer. "It's hours before you'll eat again."

Gwen didn't have to twist her arm. Jennifer selected two of the smaller pastries.

Oggie took the tray from Jennifer and happily filled his plate. "Won't force you, Irene. That just leaves more for me."

Stella took a delicate bite of pastry and a sip of wine, then glanced around the table with a look that suggested she was extremely pleased with herself. "You'll never guess what juicy tidbit I learned while I was out today."

Irene raised her eyebrows and widened her eyes. "I thought Jennifer and I were the only ones crazy enough to go out in this weather."

Stella patted her short, curly hair. "You know I never miss my weekly wash and set at the Crowning Glory, no matter what."

"It's very becoming, Stella." Oggie stopped consuming mushroom puffs long enough to offer the compliment with sincerity.

"Thank you, Oggie, dear." She leaned over and patted the man's hand, and Jennifer could have sworn he blushed.

"Anyway," Stella continued with a glow of triumph over her late-breaking gossip, "we're going to have an addition to the population of Jester."

With a muffled cry, Gwen dropped her cup of herbal tea into her saucer, shattering both.

Chapter Four

Jennifer jumped at the crash of shattering china, then grabbed a linen napkin and leaped to sop tea from the tablecloth. But Gwen, who had suddenly gone pale, waved her away.

"You all right, dear?" Irene asked with concern. "You look a bit green around the gills."

"I'm fine. Don't make a fuss. Just had a muscle spasm. Must have spent too much time this afternoon rolling out dough."

Gwen hurriedly gathered up the broken china, but Jennifer could tell her friend's hands were shaking, and her excuse had seemed forced. She wondered what had upset their usually unflappable hostess, who disappeared into the kitchen with the shattered cup and saucer. Her boarders exchanged curious and worried glances, but none questioned Gwen's explanation.

Not out loud, at least.

When Gwen returned an instant later with a fresh

cup of tea, Jennifer wondered if she'd only imagined her friend's pallor and discomfort, because she seemed her usual self again.

"What do you mean, a population increase?" Oggie asked Stella, picking up the thread of conversation. His face brightened, and he threw Jennifer a questioning look. "Have you decided to move here permanently?"

"Not much chance of that," she said ardently, remembering Luke's coolness. She could withstand the cold of the Montana winters, but his permafrost attitude had frozen too deep for comfort.

"Your staying would be very good news," Stella admitted with enthusiasm, "but this particular addition to our town is a baby."

Jennifer was watching Gwen, whose complexion appeared to blanche again, but this time she didn't drop anything. With a deadly calm voice, their hostess asked, "Who's expecting?"

Was Gwen jealous?

Jennifer had received the impression that Gwen was happy running the boardinghouse, but maybe there was more to the story. She wondered if her friend's strange reaction to a new baby in town was a sign of discontent. Did Gwen secretly long for a husband and children rather than her family of boarders?

Stella paused a dramatic moment before answering Gwen's query. "Shelly O'Rourke's expecting."

A collective intake of breaths and expressions of approval greeted her announcement.

"That's wonderful!" Irene clapped her hands together.

"Good for Shelly and Connor," Oggie stated. "They'll make wonderful parents."

"I'm happy for them," Gwen said simply, but Jennifer could tell her friend's emotions were mixed, and again wondered why.

"Vickie Perkins wrote me that Shelly had married," Jennifer admitted, "but she didn't give me many details, other than the fact that Shelly's husband is a pediatrician in Nathan's clinic."

Stella immediately launched into a lively story of how Shelly Dupree and Connor O'Rourke had been drawn together over their concern for an infant someone had abandoned in the Brimming Cup, Shelly's diner. Although the others had obviously heard the story before, they appeared to enjoy Stella's lively recap, especially Oggie, who couldn't keep his eyes off the vivacious raconteur.

With the wine working its way through her bloodstream, the warmth of the room and her companionable acceptance by the other boarders, Jennifer experienced a fresh sense of coming home. She'd been too lonely the past ten years, living by herself without family.

"Now," Stella announced, wrapping up her story, "with the abandoned baby happily back with its mother, Shelly and Connor are married and expecting a precious bundle of their own."

"So, Jennifer," Gwen said a mite too casually in changing the subject, "tell us what you've been doing since you left Jester."

Jennifer shrugged. "Nothing exciting. I've had several jobs, starting as a receptionist with a publishing house in New York. I had worked my way up to an administrative assistant, but I must still be searching for the right niche, because since then I've had jobs in Detroit, Minneapolis, Philadelphia and Chicago, and haven't put down roots yet."

"You should put them down here," Stella said emphatically. "There should always be Faulkners at Cottonwood Farm. Have been for generations."

"Absolutely," Irene agreed.

Silence filled the air for a moment, as if the room's occupants were remembering those Faulkners who had gone before.

Gwen's voice broke the quiet. "I was sorry to hear about your parents, Jenny."

The boarders murmured soothing words of consolation and sympathy over the deaths of Jennifer's parents, who had perished three years ago in a plane crash in Italy.

"Thank you," Jennifer said, touched by their condolences.

She missed her parents, but they had never been the presence in her life her grandparents had been. The only times Jennifer had spent with her mother and father had been when they picked her up at school to take her to the airport. Or met her at the airport to return her to school after vacations and holidays she'd spent in Jester. She remembered them as kind but distant strangers, always too distracted by their friends, parties and travels to pay much attention to a lonely little girl.

Irene set down her wineglass and dabbed at her lips with her napkin. "I heard a bit of news myself today."

"Good news, I hope," Oggie said. "After the pavilion collapse yesterday, we could use some good news."

Irene's expression grew thoughtful. "I guess you could call it good news, although, if it's true, we may be about to lose one of Jester's most eligible bachelors."

"Now you really have my interest," Stella said. "You can't be talking about the vet, Jack Hartman. We all saw him propose to Melinda last night, so that's not news."

"Not Jack," Irene said. "Luke McNeil."

Jennifer struggled to keep her hand steady as she placed her glass on the table. No wonder Luke had seemed so cool. Nothing like having his ex-fiancée show up just when he'd proposed to another woman.

"Luke's getting married?" Stella's eyes lighted with interest.

Irene shook her head. "As far as I know, he

hasn't popped the question, but the new woman in his life seems to think he might.''

''Don't keep us hanging,'' Stella said. ''Who's the girl?''

''Cassie Lou Carwise.''

''Don't know her,'' Oggie said with a frown. ''She's not from Jester. I know everyone who's gone through school here.''

''You're right,'' Irene said. ''Cassie Lou's from Pine Run. She works as a paralegal for Hank Durham.''

''Hank Durham?'' Jennifer's heart sank. Luke was seriously involved with someone else, a someone Jennifer would probably have to meet when she went to Durham's office to sign the papers for her grandfather's estate. All the more reason for Jennifer to finish her business and get out of town fast. It was bad enough that Luke didn't love her. She didn't want to witness his affection for Cassie Lou.

''My source,'' Irene said, obviously enjoying the impact her news was having on her fellow boarders, ''who made me swear on a stack of Bibles not to reveal her name, says that Luke has dated Cassie Lou several times. So often, in fact, Cassie Lou has started keeping a pile of *Bride* magazines on her desk. Seems she's already picking out a dress.''

''Maybe the curse is broken,'' Stella commented.

Jennifer felt her face pucker into a questioning frown. ''Curse?''

Gwen, who'd been observing Jennifer a bit too

closely for comfort, nodded. "For years, women from five counties have been throwing themselves at Luke. He's established a pattern. Dates someone once or twice, moves on to the next. Frustrates the dickens out of those who're looking for a good man to lead them to the altar."

"What's that got to do with a curse?" Jennifer asked.

Stella folded her plump arms on the table and leaned toward Jennifer, her eyes alight with intrigue. "The skinny is that someone broke Luke's heart years ago, and that he hasn't loved another woman since. Folks in Jester were beginning to think he'd be cursed by loneliness the rest of his life."

"I hope not," Oggie said emphatically. "Luke McNeil was a good boy and has turned into an exceptional man. Honest, trustworthy, slow to anger. A man you can count on in a pinch. He's kept a good many people out of serious trouble in this town. He'll make some woman a fine husband."

Gwen's expression grew thoughtful. "I had a terrible crush on Luke when I was in the fourth grade."

"You did?" Jennifer said with surprise. "I never knew that." She thought she'd been the only girl in town who'd worshipped the ground he walked on.

"He saved my life," Gwen said with a grin, "or at least I thought he had at the time."

Jennifer recalled Luke's pulling her from the creek. Maybe rescuing young girls had been his specialty. "What happened?"

Gwen, her color now back to normal, shoved her cup and saucer aside. "There was a new kid at school that year. Can't remember his name. His father was a transient, working a temporary ranch job. Anyway, this kid was big and mean, a year or two older than Luke, who must have been about sixteen then. He outweighed Luke by a good fifty pounds."

"Ah." Oggie's eyes lit with recognition. "I remember that boy."

"The bully had a racket going," Gwen said, "shaking down little kids for their lunch money. For a while, I figured I was safe because I brought my lunch to school, packed by my grandmother."

Jennifer nodded with understanding. "Then he figured out what a great cook your grandmother was."

"He made my life hell from then on. If I couldn't get to the lunchroom where Oggie was on duty before the bully stole my lunch, I went hungry for the rest of the day."

"How did Luke figure in this?" Irene asked.

"Luke caught the boy stealing my lunch one day. He just stepped up to the bully, took it from him and handed it back to me. Told the boy that what he was doing was not only hurtful to little kids, but that it was also against the law, and that if he did it again, Luke would turn him in to the sheriff. The bully never took anyone's lunch or lunch money again.''

"They didn't fight?'' Stella asked in amazement.

Oggie shook his head. "Bullies are cowards at heart. They almost always back down when confronted. But that's not the whole story. Luke came to me shortly after that incident.''

"He ratted on the bully?'' Gwen asked. "That doesn't sound like Luke.''

A gentle smile wreathed Oggie's face. "It wasn't like that at all. Luke did some investigating on his own. Found out the bully's father was gambling and drinking away all his pay. The boy was hungry. That's why he was stealing money and lunches.''

Gwen's expression turned thoughtful. "I believed he was just a rotten kid. His hunger sure puts a different spin on things.''

"But Luke did more than investigate,'' Oggie continued. "He contacted Shelly's parents at the Brimming Cup and struck a deal with them. If the boy would come in two afternoons a week and on Saturdays to help with chores, he could eat free at the diner every school day and Saturdays.''

"So what happened?'' Stella asked. "Sounds like the boy might have been too proud to take charity.''

"That's what Luke thought, too,'' Oggie said. "So he had me make the proposition to the boy as if he'd be doing the Duprees a favor. As if they were desperate for the help. Luke's always had good people skills, intuition and conflict resolution. That's what makes him such a good sheriff.''

Jennifer worked to keep her expression neutral. If Luke cared so much about people, why had he treated her so shabbily? Had she been so young and naive she'd misinterpreted his feelings all those years ago? Had she just been a summer fling? Had his talk about their future together been a lie from the beginning? Maybe her own intuition was faulty. After all, she'd never expected Grandpa Henry to disown her, but he had.

"With Luke being such a paragon, looks like Cassie Lou Carwise has grabbed the golden ring, so to speak.'' Irene drained the last of her wine. ''According to my source.''

"Is your source reliable?'' Gwen looked skeptical.

Irene shrugged. ''Only time will tell.''

Gwen rose to clear the appetizer plates away, and Jennifer took the opportunity to excuse herself. After bundling up against the cold, she slipped outside for the walk to Vickie's.

Although snow was still falling, the wind had eased. Jennifer hoped the morning would be clear. She could drive to Pine Run, sign her papers, have her car repaired and list the farm with a real estate agent. Then she'd hit the road. If she was lucky, she'd accomplish all her tasks and get out of Jester without seeing Luke again. His attitude toward her had been clearly chilly, and with Cassie Lou Carwise soon to become Mrs. Luke NcNeil, Jennifer had no desire to hang around to witness the love match.

Trudging through the high drifts, she rounded the corner at the sheriff's office on Main Street and headed toward the Perkins house, where welcoming light from every window glowed like beacons through the falling snowflakes. The picture-perfect scene of the snug house nestled in the snow filled Jennifer with regret, reminding her of the barren apartment she'd left in Chicago and the fact that she had no place, not even a temporary one, to call home. If things had worked out for her and Luke, she'd be living in a house like Vickie's now, with children of her own. The thought made her heart and arms ache with emptiness, and she struggled to put on a happy face. If she arrived looking gloomy, Vickie would eventually share that fact with Luke. The last thing Jennifer wanted was for Luke to know he'd broken her heart.

Determined to enjoy herself, Jennifer negotiated the icy front steps and rang the bell.

She didn't have to wait long in the cold. Vickie answered the door and ushered her quickly into the warmth of the living room. The family scene was just as Jennifer had imagined. Nathan was on his hands and knees in front of the fire, with only his trim, denim-clad backside visible to Jennifer. A small boy rode the man's back like a horse, a

slightly smaller girl tugged at his hair and baby
Caitlyn toddled alongside, gurgling with delight.

Vickie took Jennifer's coat. "Come out into the
kitchen and meet Nathan. Then I'll introduce you
to the kids."

Confused, Jennifer frowned. "Nathan's in the
kitchen? But I thought—"

A shriek from the boy as he tumbled from his
"horse" interrupted her, and the man in front of
the fireplace pushed to his feet and turned to face
her. Surprise registered on the strong angles of his
face and in his midnight-blue eyes.

"Jennifer?" Luke's gaze flicked accusingly to
Vickie. "You didn't tell me you were having company."

Jennifer recalled the gleam of mischief she'd
spotted on Vickie's face when she had left her
friend earlier that day, and now knew its meaning.
Vickie had known all along Luke was coming for
supper, too.

Well, if her friend intended playing matchmaker,
Jennifer had a surprise for her. No way was she
cooperating. Besides, with Luke practically engaged to Cassie Lou Carwise, Vickie had no business interfering in her brother's life.

Or Jennifer's.

But keeping her nose out of other people's business, especially that of her family and friends, had
never been Vickie's strong suit. Luckily Jennifer

wouldn't be in Jester long enough for Vickie's meddling to matter.

Fighting for composure and to keep her smile from slipping away, she said with a calm she didn't feel, "Hello again, Luke."

IF LUKE DIDN'T LOVE his scheming little sister so danged much, he'd wring her pretty conniving neck. He knelt beside six-year-old Ricky to make sure the boy hadn't hurt himself in the tumble, and was glad for the opportunity to avoid both his sister's smirk of triumph and Jennifer's barely concealed surprise.

"You mad, Uncle Luke?" Five-year-old Shannon gazed up at him through tousled curls, her brown eyes round with anxiety.

"Not me, pumpkin." He hugged her to reassure her. "Why?"

"'Cause your face is all scrunched up, like this." Shannon contorted her face into a scowl that made him laugh.

At the sound, Caitlyn attached herself to his right leg with a bear hug. "Pick me up, Wuke."

Luke scooped his younger niece into his arms, glad again for the distraction. Fresh from her bath, Caitlyn emanated that fresh baby smell that always tugged at his heartstrings and made him long for children of his own.

And whenever he thought of having children, he thought of Jennifer.

And her desertion.

The last thing he wanted tonight was to sit at his sister's table with the woman who'd left him high and dry, and make pleasant, inane conversation. If he wanted inane chatter, he'd have asked Cassie Lou for another date.

Scratch that.

He recalled the gossip that had recently run through town like a flu virus. He'd learned that Cassie Lou was so intent on matrimony, she considered a third date as good as a proposal. But he'd learned that particular piece of critical info too late—*after* the third date. He had no intention of marrying Cassie Lou, so he would avoid her from now on and cross his fingers that the rumors would die down and some other unsuspecting guy would ask her out for a third time.

No, the only woman he'd ever wanted to marry was Jennifer. Maybe her abandonment had cured him of the marriage bug for good.

He watched her disappear into the kitchen with Vickie. The graceful movements of her long, slender body, the shimmer of her stylish blond hair and the evocative scent of roses that lingered in the room made him ache with longing.

How could he still desire a woman who'd left him in the lurch without the slightest explanation? He'd never thought of himself as a masochist, but if he could still feel attracted to Jenny, he had to be one.

Cradling Caitlyn in his arms, he followed the women into the kitchen.

His brother-in-law, Nathan, stood at the counter with a freshly sliced pot roast on a carving board before him. At five-foot-nine, with hair that had gone prematurely gray, Doc looked older than his thirty-six years, which worked well for him in inspiring confidence in his patients. However, he lacked the softness that some doctors developed from too much desk work. He and Vickie and the kids loved the out-of-doors, and their outings of hiking, riding, swimming and skiing kept Doc tan and fit.

Luke suppressed an unexpected jolt of jealousy when he grasped Jennifer's hand, leaned forward and kissed her cheek.

"Vickie's told me all about you," Nathan said.

Jennifer laughed, a pleasant sound like water bubbling over rocks in the creek bed, evoking a hundred memories Luke couldn't repress.

"Not *all*, I hope," she said with an exaggerated look of horror.

"All," Nathan replied with a nod, his brown eyes twinkling. "You two were a couple of hellions, weren't you?"

"I don't know about you, Jennifer, but I haven't changed." With a wink, Vickie picked a sliver of roast from the board and popped it into her mouth.

"I always tried to be a good girl," Jennifer insisted playfully, then turned a solemn look on Vickie. "But I was surrounded by bad influences."

His sister's face split into a grin that showed how happy she was to have her old friend with her again.

"Luke?" Vickie turned to him. "Why don't you introduce Jennifer to Ricky and Shannon while Nathan and I put dinner on the table."

Vickie's expression couldn't have been sweeter or more innocent, but Luke knew exactly what was turning the wheels behind her wide-eyed look. She'd use every opportunity to throw Luke and Jennifer alone together, but her scheming was doomed. He had no intention of setting himself up for disappointment again. Besides, his boisterous nieces and nephew would form the perfect buffer against any personal conversation.

"Sure," he agreed. "C'mon, Jennifer, and meet the brat pack."

Ignoring Vickie's poorly concealed flash of victory, he returned to the living room, all too aware that Jennifer followed close behind.

Ricky was curled in the corner of the sofa, his round little face creased with concentration over the Game Boy in his hands. Shannon lay on her stomach in front of the fire, wielding a red crayon outside the lines of the figure in her coloring book.

"Ricky, Shannon," Luke said, "this is Jennifer. She's been your mom's friend since she was your age, Shannon."

"Hi." Displaying the good manners his parents

had drilled into him, Ricky set the Game Boy aside and stood to greet their visitor. His resemblance to his father was undeniable—except he was tow-headed instead of gray. Ricky had also inherited his father's sharp intelligence and his outgoing personality.

"Hello." Jennifer appeared ill at ease, and Luke couldn't tell whether he or the children were the source of her discomfort.

Shannon sat up and stared at Jennifer with interest. "Is she your friend, too, Uncle Luke?"

Trust Shannon, the bold one, to ask such a question. Luke felt the pinch of loss at her piercing inquiry. Ten years ago, before Dolly Faulkner's death, he would have answered that Jennifer was his best friend. But a decade was a long time. People could become strangers in that many years.

"We used to be friends," Jennifer said with a lightness that suggested she didn't miss the friendship as much as Luke did. "But Luke and I haven't kept in touch like your mother and I have."

"Where do you live?" Ricky asked.

"I used to live in Chicago, but right now I'm staying at Gwen Tanner's boardinghouse."

"Don't you have a home?" Shannon asked.

For a second, Luke thought he caught the glint of tears in Jennifer's eyes, then realized the room's lighting had caused the illusion when she replied with a bright smile, "Not right now. But I'm looking for one."

"Here?" Ricky asked. "You could buy this house. We're moving as soon as the new one's finished."

Luke settled into a rocker with Caitlyn asleep on his shoulder, and watched his niece and nephew grill Jennifer like pros. Maybe they'd find out what her plans were without his having to seem too interested.

Jennifer shook her head. "I won't be staying in Jester."

"Why not?" Shannon asked. "We like it here."

"It's a great place," Jennifer replied quickly, her cheeks bright with a beguiling rose hue that could have arisen from embarrassment or her proximity to the fireplace. "But I don't have family here. Or a job. Or anything else to keep me in Jester."

"Where is your family?" Ricky asked.

At that point, Luke took pity on Jennifer. "You ask too many questions, Ricky."

"I'm practicing," the boy said.

"For what?" Jennifer asked.

"To be a doctor. Daddy says you can't find out what's wrong with people unless you ask the right questions."

"Don't be silly," his sister scolded. "There's nothing wrong with Jennifer. Is there, Uncle Luke?"

Jennifer's gaze met his, and for an instant he glimpsed a deep unhappiness, before she forced a smile.

"No, Shannon," he said softly. "There's nothing wrong with Jennifer."

But something was definitely bothering her.

Although they'd been apart for years, he could still read her like a book, and with his affinity for unsolved puzzles, he found himself very curious over what was causing Jennifer's unhappiness.

Chapter Five

Seated across from Luke at the Perkinses' round dining table, an intimate and snug arrangement without its expansion leaves, Jennifer felt the desire to run.

Literally.

Running had become her passion over the last ten years, a welcome release from the loneliness and insecurity that had haunted her since her grandmother's death. Whenever the walls of whatever rented space she occupied at the time seemed to close in, Jennifer would don her running clothes, lace her Reeboks and take off, hoping to shake the gloom and depression.

Tonight she wanted to run, not from gloom and depression, but from Luke, sitting across from her as cool and distant as if they'd never planned to marry one another, as if she were some stranger his sister had just introduced.

But there was no place to run tonight. With the

roads adrift in snow, even walking was treacherous, and Jennifer knew she couldn't walk fast enough to escape the flood of memories and emotions that inundated her.

Watching Luke with his nieces and nephews, and observing his tenderness when he tucked each of them in bed to await their parents' good-night kisses, had torn at Jennifer's heart, reviving long-lost memories she'd thought she'd buried for good.

One memory in particular haunted her. It had been a night as different from tonight as possible. The warm breezes of that long-ago summer had carried the fragrance of wildflowers and prairie grasses, and the trickling music of the creek that meandered through the valley. Luke had picked up Jennifer at her grandparents in the late afternoon, and they had driven to the empty rolling prairie west of town.

Luke had taken the basket filled with the picnic supper Jennifer had packed, she grabbed a tartan blanket and they had hiked to a large sandstone outcropping that rose hundreds of feet into the sky, like a sentinel in the middle of the prairie. Laughing like children, they had scaled the minimountain and spread the tartan at the top. From their vantage point, they could spot the glint of the Yellowstone River, cutting through a distant line of trees, and the forlorn beauty of the gumbo badlands of the Sheep Mountains.

The strong breeze alleviated the summer heat as

they ate their supper, battered Stetsons shielding their heads from the descending sun, and Luke regaled her with stories of his job as a deputy, so enthusiastic over his new career and the telling that he almost forgot to eat.

Jennifer's worries over Luke's safety had temporarily marred the enjoyment of the evening.

"Aren't you in danger?" she'd asked, recalling too many televised scenes of law officers' funerals, with flag-draped coffins, bagpipe dirges and mourning families.

Luke had thrown back his head with a sharp laugh. "Not unless someone turns homicidal over a stray pig, a parking ticket or a zoning violation. I'm more likely to die of boredom."

But Jennifer knew he wasn't bored. As long as Luke was interacting with people, he would always find life interesting.

"But if trouble does come, I'm well trained for it. You mustn't worry about me. Besides—" he drew her closer and cupped her face in his hands, and his eyes danced like blue flames "—if I truly thought this job would shorten my life expectancy, we wouldn't be making the plans we've made."

"What plans?" she asked, pretending innocence to have the pleasure of hearing him recite them again.

"Next summer, we're going to have the biggest wedding Jester has ever seen, with everybody in town and half of Pine Run invited."

"And you'll wear a tuxedo?" She stifled a grin, knowing he'd balked at the idea from the start.

"Only if you hog-tie me first."

"I know a few of your friends who might be willing to lend a hand."

"Not if they want to live long and happy lives."

"And after the wedding?" Jennifer asked.

His arms tightened around her. "We're going to live to be a hundred. Together, and loving each other every day of our lives."

"You skipped a part," she teased.

"What part is that?" He nuzzled her neck with his lips, sending shivers of delight cascading through her until she almost forgot his question.

"The children," she said, when she finally managed to draw breath.

"Ah, yes. Clan McNeil. How could I forget?"

"Clan?" She pretended alarm, enjoying the game. "How many in a clan?"

His strong, capable hands skimmed from her shoulders to her wrists. He clasped her fingers in his and drew them to his lips. "As many as we want. As many as we can afford to care for properly."

An unexpected uneasiness stirred within her. "I'm not sure...."

He snapped his head up and drilled her with a worried glance. "About marrying me?"

She shook her head. "Oh, Luke, you know how

much I love you. I just worry about what kind of a mother I'll be.''

His face lightened. ''You'll be fine.''

''But I have so little experience with children. I don't have younger brothers or sisters. And at boarding school, as I grew older, we were always separated from the younger girls.''

He pulled her close again. ''I'm not worried.''

''But I've never even changed a diaper.''

''I'll teach you.''

''You know how?''

''Sure. Mom taught me to change Vickie's.''

''But you couldn't have been more than five.'' Luke's confidence in her was melting her reservations.

''Mom needed the help, and I was a quick study.'' His face was brighter than the sun lunging toward the horizon. ''And you've had more experience with children than you give yourself credit for.''

Jennifer frowned. ''Like what?''

''Like for the last four or five years, you've taken over the preschool Sunday school class—''

''But that was just when the preacher's wife went on vacation with her husband,'' Jennifer argued.

Luke continued, undeterred. ''And the rest of the time, you've been her assistant. You're great with those little kids, Jen. I've watched you. They adore you. You'll make a terrific mother.''

The tangle of anxiety unraveled within her, loosened by his confidence in her. "In that case, I want a boy who looks just like you."

"I wouldn't be unhappy if all our children look exactly like their mother."

He'd kissed her then, atop the outcropping, with the wind swirling around them, the sun setting behind the mountains and the evening star shining down like a blessing.

She opened her body and her soul to him with that kiss, feeling the length of his muscular form cleaving to hers, fiery with the heat of desire. His lips devoured hers, and his hands caressed her until she was dizzy with longing and anticipation.

"We're engaged now, Luke. We don't have to wait." She yearned to make love with him like dry ground craves water.

"Dear God, Jenny, don't tempt me."

"I'm not being coy, Luke. I want us to be together tonight."

He pulled away gently, then took her hands again and gazed into her eyes, his own filled with pain. "I can't."

Confusion struck her. He couldn't? A flurry of possible explanations filled her mind. Impotence? Not likely. Luke McNeil was the most virile man she'd ever met and he'd just voiced his expectations for children. Lack of desire? That contradicted what she read in his eyes, felt in his touch, observed in the telltale bulge of his jeans. Then her mind cleared. "If you're afraid I'll get pregnant—"

"It's not that." He cupped her face in his hands, then grazed her cheeks with his knuckles, a simple touch that stoked the already raging fire in her and turned her knees to water. "I made a promise."

"Promise?" Her confusion returned tenfold. "Like a religious vow?"

"In a way. I promised your grandfather that I wouldn't take advantage of you."

"Take advantage of me?" Her anger flared. "What am I, some incompetent who can't think for herself? I want you, Luke. Don't I have some say-so in this? After all, it's me, not Grandpa Henry, you'd be making love to."

His groan expressed more frustration than any words could relate. "I want you, too, Jennifer, in the worst—" a seductive smile creased his face "—and the best way. But I'm a man of my word. I can't break my promise to your grandfather. We'll have to wait until we're married."

A man of his word, he'd said, all those years ago....

Jennifer stole a glance at Luke across the table, carefully cutting his pot roast as if to avoid looking at her. He had kept his word to Henry, but he'd broken his promise to marry her. What kind of man did that?

And why?

"Don't you think that's a good idea?" Vickie was asking.

Jennifer shook off her memories. Across the table, Luke had assumed the uncomfortable demeanor of a nocturnal animal frozen in a sudden bright light.

"Sorry, Vickie," Jennifer admitted. "What were you saying?"

"You mentioned you're having car trouble, right?"

Jennifer relaxed, happy for a neutral subject, but wondering why her car problem had spooked Luke. "I called Tex's Garage and explained what it's doing."

"Tex probably wasn't much help," Nathan said. "He works mostly on farm equipment and older cars."

"That's what he told me," Jennifer replied. "He suggested I take my car into the dealership in Pine Run. Something about computerized diagnostics. But with the snowstorm, the road's impassable."

"But the weather will clear tomorrow, won't it?" Vickie asked Luke.

He broke open a biscuit and slathered it with butter. "The storm's moving out. The crews will work all night and have the road open by morning."

Vickie nodded with satisfaction. "That will work just fine, then, won't it, Jennifer?"

Apparently she had missed more of the conversation than she'd realized. "What will work just fine?"

"Luke has to go to Pine Run in the morning," Vickie said, so casually Jennifer was sure her friend had plotted her response long and hard. "He can follow you in to make sure your car arrives at the dealership, then give you a ride back."

Luke took a bite of biscuit and chewed, but said nothing.

"I can't impose on Luke." The thought of being closed up in a car with him for the ride back from Pine Run made Jennifer feel suddenly panicky.

As if sensing her distress, Nathan reached over and patted her hand. "You won't be imposing if Luke's making the trip anyway, will she, Luke?"

Luke swallowed his mouthful of biscuit, his expression unfathomable. "To serve and protect, that's our motto. Giving you a lift back from Pine Run is part of the service."

Jennifer's heart sank. She could tell Luke was just being polite, that probably the last thing he wanted was being cooped up alone with her on the drive back from Pine Run, but there was no way she could turn down his suggestion without looking petulant and childish.

Feeling as if her face would crack from her forced smile, she nodded. "Thanks, Luke. I appreciate the offer."

Offer, my foot, Jennifer thought with a twinge of annoyance at Vickie's clever maneuvering. Her friend had backed them both into a box neither could escape from.

"Good," Vickie said, with nothing fake about

her wide grin of satisfaction. ''Now that's settled, who wants dessert?''

LUKE HAD BEEN RIGHT on the money about the weather. The next morning dawned clear, and so bright Jennifer had to dig her sunglasses out of her purse in preparation for the drive to Pine Run.

As she approached her car, her heart swelled with gratitude toward Finn Hollis. He apparently intended to take his old friend's granddaughter under his wing, because he'd sent his grandson Seth to the boardinghouse long before sunrise. Not only had the lanky nineteen-year-old dug her car out of a drift; he'd also used a snowblower to clear a path to the street.

Praying that whatever was affecting her car would allow it to reach Pine Run before breaking down completely, Jennifer eased the sedan down the drive and onto Main Street. Thankful for the snow tires that gripped the icy road, she parked alongside the curb behind Luke's dark SUV, with its prominent Sheriff markings, light bar and grill-work separating the front seat from the rear. She couldn't help wondering how many dangerous felons, if any, he'd driven to jail confined to that back seat.

A work crew was busy clearing snow from the sidewalks as Jennifer left her car and walked to the sheriff's office, a change from the old days when snow lay until it melted or folks wore their own paths. Maybe Mayor Bobby Larson's intentions to put Jester on the map were behind the rapid-response cleanup efforts.

Drawing a deep breath and gathering her courage for her next encounter with Luke, Jennifer shoved open the door of the sheriff's office and stepped inside. Warm, dry air greeted her, and she closed the door quickly behind her to prevent its escape.

The room was small and utilitarian. Beige walls, pine desk and chairs, filing cabinets and a dilapidated table that held a coffeemaker and a supply of foam cups were the room's only furnishings. Gouges and scuff marks covered the hardwood floors, especially thick near the door that led to the jail cell, as if soon-to-be prisoners had dragged their feet. The room smelled of pine cleaner, with a hint of Luke's citrus-scented aftershave.

Luke glanced up from the file spread open on the desk in front of him, and her heart twisted at the sight of him. The years had made him more handsome, if anything, but even at thirty-three, not a trace of gray was evident in his coal-black hair. The tiny lines at the corners of his eyes added character to his face, and his wide generous mouth made her ache with memories of his kisses.

''Ready?'' he asked in a nonchalant tone.

For a moment, she feared he had read her mind. She was ready, all right. Ready to throw herself into his arms and beg him to love her again. Then reason and pride shook her out of her impossible day-dream.

"No hurry," she said. "I can fit my schedule to yours."

"I have several errands in Pine Run." His voice remained almost toneless. "It might be afternoon before I head back here."

"Suits me. I have several stops to make. If I'm lucky, my car might even be ready by then."

The impersonal level of their exchange depressed her. She recalled conversations from the past where the atmosphere had zinged with electricity and witty repartee, sparked by the attraction that had hovered between them.

Before he could rise from his desk, his phone rang. "Sheriff's office."

From the scowl on his face, Jennifer could tell Luke wasn't happy about the call.

"Okay, Bobby, I'll be down in a minute." Luke grimaced at the caller's reply, then answered, "Sure, Robert, if that's what you want."

He slammed the phone into its cradle, pushed back from his desk and reached for his coat.

"Trouble?" Jennifer asked.

"Pain in the neck," Luke muttered. "I have to run down to the town hall for a few minutes. I've been summoned by His Honor."

"The mayor?"

"None other." Luke shrugged into his coat and slammed on his Stetson. "I swear the man's developed delusions of grandeur ever since the lottery win.''

''And he really makes you call him Robert?''

The tightness in Luke's face relaxed and he almost smiled. ''He tries. Look, why don't you have a cup of coffee at the Brimming Cup, and I'll meet you there when the mayor's through with me.''

''Sure.'' Relief cascaded through her. Anything to avoid the tension between them a few minutes longer.

Luke opened the door for her, and she preceded him out into the sunshine. He walked alongside her, shortening his long-legged stride to match hers. When she stepped off the curb to cross Big Draw Drive, her foot slipped on the ice, and only Luke's firm grip kept her from crashing to the ground. He'd clasped his arms around her to stop her fall, and she found herself pressed against the soft suede of his jacket. His familiar male scent filled her nostrils, rocking her with nostalgia.

She'd forgotten how good his arms around her felt, how much she loved the smell of him, and she had to force herself to push away, when all she wanted was to bury herself deeper in his embrace.

What was the matter with her?

The man was an old flame, nothing more, and now practically engaged to someone else. With her cheeks burning with embarrassment as well as cold, she avoided his gaze. ''Thanks for the save.''

''Serve and protect, remember.'' His words were

casual, but the slight catch in his voice made her wonder if their contact had affected him as much as it had her.

"Good thing there's not much traffic in Jester," he said lightly.

"What?"

"We'd both have been run over by now."

She almost slipped again in her haste to get off the street, and Luke gripped her elbow until she was safely on the sidewalk in front of the barbershop.

"Can you make it across Main Street all right?" he asked.

Her face flamed again. "Sure. I'm not as old and feeble as I look."

He started to say something, then closed his mouth and nodded toward the diner. "Then I'll meet you there as soon as I can get away from the mayor."

Without a backward glance, he turned and trudged up the street toward the town hall.

Before Jennifer headed for the diner, she caught sight of Finn Hollis through the barbershop window. Will Devlin was sprawled in the barber's chair, and Dean Kenning was giving him a trim. Finn sat in one of the waiting chairs, a battered copy of *Time* magazine in his hands.

Jennifer rapped on the glass and beckoned to Finn when he glanced her way. She knew better than to enter that bastion of maleness, considered off-limits to the females of Jester. Meeting his

cronies had been one of her grandfather's favorite
pastimes, but he had always admonished her never
to enter, but to knock on the window if she needed
him. Dean waved a greeting with the hand that held
the scissors, then went back to his barbering. Finn
pushed himself to his feet and headed for the door.

Outside on the sidewalk, he enveloped her in a
hug. "You haven't changed a bit, Jenny, even
though I haven't seen you for several months of
Sundays."

She returned his embrace, savoring the warmth
and inhaling the scent of English Leather, old books
and pipe tobacco that had clung to the man as long
as she'd known him. Finn had always been like a
member of the family. "It's good to see you, Uncle
Finn. Thank you for sending Seth over this morning. I'd still be digging out my car without his
help."

"I'd have done it myself," Finn said, "but I'm
not as young as I used to be."

"You look wonderful." Jennifer meant every
word. Except for the whiteness of his hair, the thin,
lanky retired librarian appeared exactly as she remembered him from her childhood days, when she
and Vickie would escape the summer heat in the
coolness of the stacks of the library. Finn had always had just the right story to recommend, and he
had nurtured in them—and every child in Jester—
a love of books and reading.

Moisture gathered in his eyes. "That's sweet of

you to say so. And you—you look so much like
your grandmother it's uncanny.''

"Thanks, Uncle Finn. That's one of the nicest
things anyone could ever say to me." She remembered Luke used to tell her the same thing.

Jennifer glanced up the street after Luke. His
long-legged stride ate up the pavement, reminding
her of the heroic lawmen of the reruns of old West-
erns she'd watched as a kid. Over six feet tall, with
broad shoulders, narrow hips and a subtle confidence, he was an imposing presence, one she was
certain folks in Jester found comforting, knowing
he was safeguarding their lives and belongings. Just
being near Luke had always made her feel safe,
secure. Treasured. She pushed the old emotions and
the longings they created away. That had been another life, another time that she would never capture
again.

She noted that Luke hadn't yet reached the town
hall, and she could be in for a long wait. She turned
back to Finn. "Let me buy you a cup of coffee.
You can tell me all about your family."

At the door of the diner, Shelly, looking pretty
and healthy in the first blush of her pregnancy,
greeted them cheerfully, showed them to a booth
and poured them cups of steaming coffee.

"Come by the house while you're here, Jenny,"
she invited. "We have a lot to catch up on. And I
want you to meet Connor."

Once Shelly had left them alone, Finn ran

through the activities of his children and grandchildren, who had kept his life full and active since
the death of his wife, Hester, twenty years earlier.
Finally Jennifer broached a subject that had
weighed on her mind for the last ten years.

"Tell me about Grandpa Henry, Finn."

He reached across the table and gently squeezed
her hand. "He died peacefully, in his sleep."

"You told me that in your letter. I want to know
about the last years of his life, after I left Jester."

Finn shook his head sadly. "Henry was a sad
case. First Dolly's death, then your leaving... You
broke his heart, Jenny."

"*I* broke his heart? Uncle Finn, he threw me
out!" Jennifer clasped a hand over her mouth in
horror. She hadn't meant to tell her awful secret,
but at the unfairness of Finn's accusation, the words
had flown out, of their own accord.

Shock registered clearly on the old man's face.
"I can't believe that."

Indignation burned through her. "Do you think
I'd lie about something that terrible?"

Finn squeezed her hand again. "Of course not.
You've always told the truth." He paused, as if
trying to assimilate what she'd told him. "Why did
he make you leave? An argument?"

She shook her head. "We never exchanged a
cross word. The day after Gramma's funeral he told
me I had to go and never come back. He wouldn't
say why. I was hoping you could tell me."

Finn scratched his head, and the fine lines of his face settled into a perplexed expression. "That just doesn't sound like Henry. But then he was never the same after your grandmother's death."

"How?"

Finn dumped extra sugar into his coffee and swirled it with his spoon. "He rarely smiled, even at a good joke. Lost all interest in the farm—and his appearance. Most of the time, he looked like a vagrant. Didn't eat. Couldn't sleep."

"Grieving?" Jennifer felt her heart clench with guilt. Her grandfather had been terribly unhappy, and she hadn't been there to help him through his sorrow.

Finn sipped his coffee, then shook his head. "He mourned your grandmother, but it went deeper than that. I think it was a deep depression he couldn't shake."

Jennifer wrapped her cold hands around her cup to warm them, but nothing could shake the chill in her heart at the image of her grandfather's unhappiness.

"I'm no therapist," Finn continued, "but I read every book on depression I could get my hands on, and Henry had all the symptoms. I tried to get him to talk to Doc Perkins. Figured one of those new antidepressants might perk him up, but Henry flat-out refused. Said pills couldn't undo what bothered him. That nothing could undo it now."

"Did he ever talk about me?"

The old man's shoulders slumped. "I wish I could tell you otherwise. At first I tried to convince him to contact you, but he wouldn't."

"Grandpa always did have a stubborn streak," she said, "but it was usually more endearing than irritating."

"Well, he irritated me plenty when he wouldn't get in touch with you. Then he outright refused to talk about you at all. I would have tried to shake some sense into him, but he was so blue I couldn't stay angry with him for long."

Jennifer fought back tears. "So Grandpa was unhappy all those years until he died?"

As if lost in the past, Finn gazed out across the street, squinting in the early-morning sunlight glinting off the shop windows. "Some days he seemed almost his old self. He still hung out at the barbershop every day. I think being with his friends, especially Dean and me, kept him going."

"But nothing really cheered him up after Gramma died?"

"There was one thing," Finn admitted, returning his gaze to hers. "Henry was tickled pink about winning the Big Draw."

Jennifer frowned. "That doesn't sound like Grandpa. He never cared much about money as long as he had enough to pay the bills."

Finn nodded. "He was so elated, I was curious. Asked him how he planned to spend his winnings. His eyes teared up then, and his hands shook. 'This will go a ways toward paying off a debt I owe,' he told me, looking like he wanted to bawl.''

"What debt?" Jennifer asked. "He invested the income from the sale of his hardware store after he retired. And he owned his farm free and clear. Even if he hadn't, that property's not worth one million dollars, much less two, so the debt can't be a mortgage.''

"He never would elaborate, and I didn't press him. A man's money is his own business, I always say.''

"Whatever the debt was, he never paid it," Jennifer said. "According to Hank Durham, Grandpa's attorney, he never got around to spending his winnings. He left everything to me—unless someone has a claim against his estate that I don't know about.''

Finn grimaced. "I doubt that. If there's a claim, we'd have read about it in that ghastly gossip column in the *Pine Run Plain Talker.* No one can sneeze in this town lately without being written up in that rag the next day.''

"Maybe whoever Grandpa owed hasn't come forward yet," Jennifer said.

"Could be." Finn drained his cup and signaled Shelly for a refill. "Henry apparently had a lot of secrets he never shared with anyone. I'd never have guessed in a million years that he turned his own granddaughter out.''

After all that time, Jennifer still suffered pain at

her grandfather's rejection. "It's been ten years, and I still can't believe it."

Suddenly she sensed Luke's presence, as if an internal radar attuned to him had alerted her, even before she caught sight of his approach out of the corner of her eye. She glanced up to find him standing at the edge of the table, nodding a greeting to Finn.

"Hey, Luke," Finn said. "What's the law up to these days?"

"Trying to strike a balance between doing my job and keeping the mayor happy," Luke replied with a scowl.

Jennifer guessed the meeting at city hall hadn't gone well, but before she or Finn could ask any questions, Luke was turning to leave.

"Ready?" His deep, pleasant voice rumbled in her ears, the sensation setting off another deluge of memories and longing.

Wondering how she'd survive the return from Pine Run in Luke's company as a stranger instead of the woman he loved, Jennifer said goodbye to Finn and followed Luke from the diner.

Her thoughts whirled as she climbed into her car, and she breathed a sigh of relief when it started without difficulty. She was anxious to reach Pine Run. Maybe Hank Durham knew to whom her grandfather was indebted. Not that Jennifer cared about his money. As alluring as the prospect of being a millionaire might be, what she really wanted was an explanation her grandfather might have left her, one that finally revealed why he'd sent her away ten years ago.

Chapter Six

The faint but unmistakable subtle rose fragrance of Jennifer's perfume was driving Luke crazy, stirring up old memories, igniting old passions. If the outside temperature hadn't been in the teens, he would have rolled down the windows of the SUV to disperse the exquisite torture.

Jennifer sat on the front seat beside him, oblivious to the havoc she was wreaking on his psyche as they returned from their day in Pine Run.

He'd hoped the mechanic at the dealership could repair her car in a few hours so she could drive herself back, saving Luke this forced encounter, but no such luck. A part had to be ordered from Billings and would take two working days to arrive. With the weekend looming, Jennifer faced four days without a car. From now on, however, Luke swore to himself, if his conniving sister wanted her friend chauffeured somewhere, she could drive her herself.

More than anything, Luke wanted to ask Jennifer

why she'd left without a word all those years ago, but his pride wouldn't let him. No man wanted to risk hearing that he simply hadn't mattered in the life of the woman he'd loved.

Thinking about the past was driving him nuts, so he turned to conversation. "Get everything done you needed to?"

Jennifer nodded. "After I left my car at the garage, I went to Hank Durham's office to sign the papers for Grandpa's estate."

Luke stifled a groan. Cassie Lou Carwise was Hank's paralegal, and he couldn't help wondering if she was still spreading the rumor of her imminent engagement to Luke. Not that it mattered whether Jennifer had heard the gossip. She wouldn't be hanging around long enough to know—or care— one way or the other. Her next words confirmed that.

"And I went by the real estate agency to inquire about listing the farm."

"Sounds like you covered all the bases." He tried to keep the bitterness from his voice. At one time, Jennifer had sworn she wanted to spend the rest of her days in Jester. With him. Now it appeared she couldn't get out of town fast enough. "As soon as your car's fixed, you can make tracks."

From the periphery of his vision, he could see her face scrunch in the delightful expression she'd always assumed when something troubled her. The sight made him want to pull the car over and kiss her senseless right then and there, but he reined in his galloping emotions, reminding himself that if he tried, she'd probably knock him senseless for his efforts.

"I'd planned to leave as soon as my car's ready—until I talked to the real estate agent," she admitted.

"What's the delay? Paperwork?"

"More like hard labor," she said with a sigh.

"You've lost me," he said.

"The Realtor said if Grandpa's farm's not in tip-top shape, not only won't I get the best price, but in an economically depressed area like Jester, it might not sell at all."

"The farm's in pretty bad condition," Luke said gently, hoping to ease the blow. "I was the one who found Henry's body. When he didn't show up at the barbershop that morning, Finn was worried. Had me drive out to check on him."

Luke had loved the old man and still mourned his loss. Finding him stone cold in his bed had grieved Luke deeply.

"You were saying about the farm?" Jennifer prodded, making Luke realize a long moment of silence had hung between them while he remembered his old friend with sadness.

"Your grandmother would be spinning in her grave if she knew what a mess the place is. I don't think Henry lifted a finger there after she died."

''Sounds like I have my work cut out for me,'' Jennifer said, a little too brightly, as if covering her true feelings. ''Good thing I took time to stop by the utility offices to have the electricity and phone turned on. With that much work needed, I'll probably live at the farm until it's ready to show for sale.''

Hope swelled inside of him, only to be doused by his own common sense. How long Jennifer stayed in Jester didn't matter. If he hadn't won her heart ten years ago, he wasn't going to win it now. Not when she'd already expressed her intentions of leaving town ASAP. She'd made it clear she had nothing to hold her here, especially not him.

''How did your day go?'' she asked in an interested tone, though he guessed she was just being polite. ''Sounded like you got off to a bad start with the mayor.''

''That pompous—'' Luke bit back the descriptive noun, which wasn't appropriate for mixed company. ''What he doesn't know about law enforcement would fill southeastern Montana.''

''He's giving you grief?'' she asked in a sympathetic way that reminded him what a good listener she'd always been, one of the many qualities he'd found so endearing.

Going down memory lane was too painful and futile, so he jerked his thoughts back to Bobby Larson. Technically, the mayor was his boss, and Luke never ran down the man to anyone, no matter how

angry he made him. But Bobby had pushed Luke
to his limit today, and he needed the opportunity to
vent his anger. Jennifer had never been a gossip,
and she'd be leaving town soon, anyway, so he responded to her offer of a sympathetic ear.

"The day before you arrived, the pavilion collapsed," Luke began.

"I heard about that at the boardinghouse. Surely
the mayor's not blaming you?"

Luke shook his head. "Not directly, no. As soon
as it happened, I marked off the area as a crime
scene—"

"You think someone destroyed the place on purpose?"

He shrugged. "I'm no construction expert, but
my instincts tell me something's fishy about the
way that structure came down."

"And the mayor disagrees?"

"The mayor doesn't care why the pavilion fell."
Luke felt his earlier anger welling up again. "All
he cares about is having it repaired as soon as possible. He doesn't want the unsightly wreckage mar-
ring the town image."

"The town image?" Jennifer giggled. "Jester
has a town image?"

The delightful sound of her laughter cooled the
anger boiling inside him. "Silly, isn't it? But the
mayor is determined our town is meant for bigger
and better things. And a collapsed pavilion in the
town park is an eyesore he can't endure."

"So you're letting them clear the wreckage?"

"No way. I told him if he tried, I'd arrest him for obstruction of justice and interfering with an investigation."

"I'm sure that didn't make him happy," she said with a worried look.

"I intend to avoid him for a few days. Give him time to cool off. One of my errands today was at the Pine Run Construction Company. I got the name of a structural engineer in Billings who'll come inspect the damage. I could be wrong, but before I take that crime scene tape down, I want every assurance that the collapse *was* an accident. If it wasn't, I don't want the evidence destroyed."

"Jester's lucky to have you, Luke." Her throaty voice caressed him, soothing his irritation over the mayor's heavy-handedness. "You take your responsibilities seriously, and that helps keep people safe."

Her words touched him, because Jenny had never been one to dish out compliments lightly. Sincerity was another of her qualities he'd valued.

"My other errand wasn't quite as successful," he admitted, warming to her company and glad for a chance to talk about the worry that had troubled him since the lottery win. "If I tell you about it, will you keep it to yourself?"

"Cross my heart."

A single glance at her assured him his secrets were safe with her. Jennifer might have broken his heart, but she was as honest and trustworthy as the stock she came from. If she promised not to divulge his secret, he could count on her discretion.

"I tried to get the county to assign me another deputy," he admitted.

"Because of the pavilion?"

"That I could handle on my own," he said. "It's the lottery winnings that concern me. When the Main Street Millionaires were first announced, Jester was flooded with media, and I was assigned an additional deputy for crowd control. Then the brouhaha died down, and he was recalled."

"The town seems pretty quiet," Jennifer said, "but I arrived in the middle of a blizzard, so maybe it's livelier than it appears."

"I'm not concerned about crowds or media now," Luke explained. "I'm concerned about our millionaires."

"People in Jester don't strike me as the type to raise a lot of sand," Jennifer said with a teasing edge to her voice. "The winners aren't likely to cause you much trouble."

Luke laughed. "You've got it all backward. I don't expect the winners to make trouble. But I do want to be on guard against anyone who might make trouble for them." He paused and glanced at her, meeting those tropical-sea-blue eyes before returning his attention to the road. "Guess you're included in that elite group now, too, what with Henry's leaving you his winnings."

"You expecting another media blitz?"

Uneasiness had crept into her tone, and he recalled what a shy and private person she'd always been. The glare of publicity would make her miserable.

He shook his head. "The press has pretty much milked this story for all it's worth. It's the criminal element that worries me. With all the nationwide attention the Main Street Millionaires have had, every scumbag in the country knows Jester is filled with people with lots of money."

"I suppose most of that money's deposited in the Jester Savings and Loan," Jennifer said. "Isn't it safe enough there?"

"If bank robbers are all we're dealing with."

"What else is there?"

Luke's gut tightened as he considered the possibilities. "People with big bucks are targets for kidnappers, blackmailers, scam artists. Any lowlife who wants to get his hands on someone else's money."

"Kidnappers," Jennifer said with a gasp. "You don't think Vickie's children are in danger?"

He flashed her a reassuring smile. "I tend to err on the side of caution. That's why I want another deputy, to help keep track of the comings and goings of any strangers or new people in town. I figure if troublemakers know they're being watched, they'll be less likely to try something, and will eventually move on to easier prey."

"Will you get your deputy?"

"They're thinking about it," he said with a scowl, "which essentially means no."

"I'm sorry, Luke." Her face brightened. "Maybe you could deputize a few of the towns-people—unofficially, that is. Nobody passes down Main Street without Dean Kenning and Finn Hollis spotting them and taking note. They could be your extra sets of eyes and ears."

"Not a bad idea," Luke said, throwing her an admiring glance.

The stunning smile she cast him in return dazzled him, sending his memories spinning back over the years.

The early summer of the year he'd fallen in love with Jennifer, he'd taken his two weeks of vacation and spent every waking moment with her. One day, they'd left before dawn and driven to Glendive, where the Chamber of Commerce offered guided boat tours on the Yellowstone River, specifically designed for agate hunting.

Ever since Jennifer had begun visiting her grand-parents as a child, she'd shown an intense interest in her adopted state. Luke could recall her pumping Vickie for details of state history that his sister had learned in school. Vickie had hated the subject, but Jenny had always lamented that the only state she knew anything about was Connecticut, where her fancy boarding school was located.

As a special treat that summer day, Luke had

decided to teach Jennifer about the famous moss agates of Montana, found along the banks of the Yellowstone River.

"If you remember your geography," he explained, "the Yellowstone starts at the mouth of the Bighorn and runs northeast until it joins the Missouri. It passes through gravel beds rich with semi-precious stones, especially sapphires and moss agates—"

"The official gemstones of Montana," Jennifer said with a complacent expression. "I'm not totally ignorant about the state."

"The moss agates are hard to spot in the rough because of their matte, yellowish exterior," Luke said. "You don't see their translucence until they're sliced open."

"And we're up at the crack of dawn and headed for Glendive because…?" Jennifer asked sleepily. She had admitted when he picked her up in the early-morning darkness that she wasn't a morning person, more of a night owl than a lark, and that anything that early except a warm bed left her grumpy and testy.

"To find agates," Luke said patiently.

"There's a basketful on the counter at the Mercantile," Jennifer said. "All you have to do is buy one."

"That takes all the fun out of it," he replied.

"Getting up in the dead of night, then enduring blazing sun, backbreaking searches of riverbeds, sunburn, insect bites…'' Jennifer grumbled drowsily. ''Did I really agree to this yesterday?''

''Yes, you did, and while you were complaining just now, you left out the glory of the hunt and the triumph of success.''

Jennifer yawned. ''Find a place that sells hot, black coffee by the gallon, and I may forgive you for cutting short my sleep.''

''Trust me,'' Luke said, ''you'll thank me for this one day.''

Jennifer made a face at him, but laughter sparkled in her eyes. ''Isn't that what parents say just before punishing their children?''

After a stop at the hotel restaurant in Wibaux for breakfast and a much-needed infusion of caffeine, her usual sweet nature returned. By the time they'd headed on toward Glendive, her enthusiasm for their day trip had returned, too.

''How did you become interested in agate hunting?'' she asked.

''My college roommate was a walking encyclopedia on the subject,'' Luke explained. ''Did you know that moss agates occur almost exclusively in the Yellowstone Valley?''

''I do now.'' She grinned at him. ''And I have a feeling I'm about to learn more about moss agates than I ever wanted to know.''

''Just stop me if you're bored,'' he said, ''but I don't think you will be. It's fascinating how agates are formed. They originate in volcanic ash and lava beds. Gases form bubbles in the cooling rock, and these holes fill with water carrying silica solutions tinted with mineral traces. As these solutions harden, they form bands of color. Moss agates are special, because as they harden, small fractures allow plumelike formations of silica in the stone, creating the appearance of a mini-landscape, with images of trees or sunsets or lakes. That's why they're also called picture agates.''

''I think my eyes just glazed over from information overload,'' Jennifer said, pretending boredom, but he could tell she was interested. She had an insatiable curiosity for new experiences.

A few hours later, those same eyes widened with delight when they located their first agate, which Luke cracked open to reveal the exotic beauty of its translucent interior.

At noon, they withdrew from the others on the tour into the shade of the cottonwoods and settled on a large boulder to eat their boxed lunches. Overhead, a golden eagle floated on an updraft, watching for rabbits and mice, and a breeze off the river cooled their skin, alleviating the summer heat.

''Having fun, sunshine?'' he asked.

''Absolutely,'' Jennifer answered immediately, quelling any doubts generated by her early-morning grumblings. ''It's a gorgeous day. The company's terrific. And the agates are spectacular.''

''That big one is yours, to remember today by.''

Her slender hands caressed the agate, not only

the biggest but also the most impressive stone that he'd found. The silica tracings had created the image of a weeping willow by the side of a lake.

"We'll find us a spot just like that, build our house and raise our children." Hope and anticipation filled him. "We've got our whole lives ahead of us, sunshine."

"Luke?" She'd tilted her head and gazed at him with questioning eyes. A tiny frown creased her forehead, and he resisted the urge to smooth it with his finger. "Why do you call me 'sunshine'?"

Because you light up my life. You make me happy when skies are gray. You warm my heart. You brighten my days.

The phrases were obvious clichés, but he felt every word of them in his heart. He'd never met another woman like Jennifer, who made him feel as if half of him had been missing until he'd found her, making the two of them one perfect whole. But how could he tell her all those things without sounding foolish? And especially with a boatload of tourists yards away who might overhear.

"Your hair reminds me of sunlight," he'd said, and changed the subject.

But he'd told her later, one night while they lay in the bed of his pickup truck on the prairie, snuggled in the warmth of a blanket while they watched the stars. He'd almost held his breath for fear she'd laugh at his sentimentality, and her reaction had stunned him.

She'd cried. Tears of happiness.

If he'd had any doubts about whether they were meant for each other, when she wrapped her arms around his neck and shed warm tears of joy on the front of his shirt, not the slightest misgiving remained.

That's why her ultimate desertion had blindsided him, left him reeling and confused.

And angry.

Had he been so infatuated, so crazy in love that he'd missed obvious signs that Jennifer hadn't been sincere? He wondered now. And if not, what the hell had happened?

He squelched the urge to stop the SUV and shake an explanation from her. Not a wise move for any man, and certainly not for the sheriff of Jester.

Her next questions distracted him from his anger. "Who are the other Main Street Millionaires? There're so many I can't keep them straight. And do you think any of them are particularly vulnerable to the lowlifes you're worried about?"

He exhaled slowly to ease his repressed anger before replying. "Besides Nathan and Vickie, there's Shelly Dupree. Shelly O'Rourke now."

"Shelly deserved to win," Jennifer said with an emphatic nod. "She's worked hard at the diner ever since she was a little girl. And you probably don't need to worry about her. Shelly's too smart to be taken in by con artists, unless she's changed a lot from the way I remember her."

"We all change." He couldn't keep the sharp edge from his voice. "But you're right, Shelly's a bright woman, and her husband didn't get to be a pediatrician without plenty of equipment in the brains department."

"Finn's no slouch either when it comes to smarts," Jennifer said, "but he does have all those grandchildren." She shivered, as if imagining the same scenarios that had kept Luke awake nights since the Big Draw win.

"I'll put a bug in Finn's ear," Luke said. "Warn him to have his family be on the lookout for anyone suspicious."

"Dean Kenning won, too, didn't he? I remember seeing him in the newscasts in Chicago."

Luke nodded. "Dean can look out for himself. And he doesn't have any family. Although there have been a few rumors...."

"What kind of rumors?"

Luke pictured the jovial, heavily built barber, who was in his mid-sixties, with dyed-brown hair. He hoped the stories he'd heard were true. Dean was a great guy. He deserved someone special in his life. "Folks say he did more than just play the lottery on his weekly trips to Pine Run. According to the local gossip mills, he has a lady friend there."

"Does he still live above the barbershop?"

"As of now. I haven't heard how he plans to spend his windfall, but he's lived so many years with the same lifestyle, I can't picture him changing his ways now, in spite of all that money.''

Luke gazed at the road ahead, the shoulders piled several feet high with drifts left by the snowplows. The thick blanket of white on the adjacent fields gave a monotony to the landscape that left him disoriented for a moment, wondering where he was. Then he spotted a familiar barn in the distance and regained his bearings.

''Will Devlin is another winner I guess I don't need to worry about,'' he said, returning to his list of Main Street Millionaires. ''Dev's not the hellraiser he once was, but he's used to handling trouble in his business. The only person likely to give him grief is Amanda Bradley. Dev can look out for himself.''

''I remember,'' Jennifer admitted. ''No one messed with him, not even when he was a kid.''

Wondering what else she remembered, Luke added another name to the millionaire list. ''Jack Hartman also won.''

''I don't know Jack Hartman.''

''He's a relative newcomer. One of our resident vets.''

''Is he the one about to be married?''

Luke nodded. ''He's a widower. His wife died in a car accident five years ago. No children. Now he's about to tie the knot again.''

''I heard his fiancée's name at the boardinghouse, but she isn't anyone I know.''

"His associate, Melinda Woods. She's new in town, too."

Luke had named over half the millionaires, and as he discussed them with Jennifer, some of his fears faded. They were a savvy group, not the type likely to be duped by scam artists or caught unawares by criminals. Still, he'd feel a lot better about security with an extra deputy.

"And, of course, you know that Gwen Tanner was a winner," he added.

Jennifer nodded. "Gwen's so down-to-earth. Except for new kitchen appliances, you'd never know she's just come into a fortune."

"Then there's Kyle and Olivia Mason."

"Does Olivia still teach?" Jennifer asked.

"Yep, and still ranks up there as everybody's favorite grade school teacher in Jester. Has for almost twenty years."

"Everyone knows how much she loves children. Did she and Kyle ever have kids of their own?"

"Never did." Her question set off a flood of sadness in Luke, reminding him of the children he and Jennifer had talked of having.

Children who would never be born.

Luke abandoned his painful thoughts. "Honor Lassiter was a winner, too."

"I remember her. She's just a few years older than me. I always thought she was gorgeous. She's never married?"

Luke shook his head.

"The boys were always lining up at her door," Jennifer said. "I figured one of them would have proposed by now."

Luke had gone out with Honor a few times after Jennifer left him, but he and Honor had been good friends, nothing more. "Seems she's been unlucky in the relationship department."

"Let's just hope some jerk out for her money doesn't steal her heart," Jennifer said forcefully. "Even an extra deputy can't protect her from that."

Lordy, that brought up a problem Luke hadn't contemplated. If he let Jennifer know he still cared for her, would she think he was just after her fortune? *No problem,* he reminded himself. The woman obviously wanted nothing to do with him, regardless of his motives.

Jennifer was counting on her fingers. "That's ten winners. Who had the other two winning tickets?"

"Sylvia Rutledge had one."

"What's Sylvia up to these days?"

"Owns the Crowning Glory Hair Salon," Luke said, "and has a steady stream of customers—when she's not out of town at some hair convention. She and Gwen Tanner are good buddies, so you'll probably run into her while you're staying at Gwen's."

Jennifer slid her fingers through her hair, triggering Luke's memories of his own fingers entwined in that soft silkiness. "I may need to visit her shop if I'm here much longer. And who's the final winner?"

"Ruby and Sam Cade."

"They're back in town? I thought Sam was in the army and they lived on base."

"Air Force," Luke explained. "And he's still on active duty. Ruby came back to Jester a few years ago. She co-owns the Mercantile with Honor."

"The Cades are separated?"

Luke shrugged. "No one knows for sure, and Ruby doesn't talk about it."

"I hope things work out for them, but there are some situations even a million dollars can't fix."

Ain't that the truth, Luke thought. All the money in the world wouldn't explain why Jennifer had walked out on him, why the love he'd thought would last a lifetime had apparently fizzled overnight. "Can't buy me love," as the Beatles' song went.

Suddenly he had the urge to drown his problems in a good stiff drink, and thought longingly of the Heartbreaker Saloon. Aptly named. But all the beer Roy Gibson, Dev's Willy-Nelson-look-alike bartender, could draw wouldn't answer Luke's questions, make Jennifer love him again, or ease the pain in his heart.

But tying one on could lose him his job, so he abandoned the idea.

He stole a glance at Jennifer's profile, cool and elegant, and wondered if she had any regrets over leaving him. But such speculation was useless. The sooner he could lose himself in his work and push memories and longings from his mind, the better. With relief, he caught sight of Jester at the next rise of the road.

In a few moments, he could drop Jennifer at Gwen's boardinghouse, and his exquisite torture would be ended.

Maybe.

Chapter Seven

The morning after her trip to Pine Run dawned bright and clear and thirty degrees warmer, but Jennifer's mind was still fogged with questions. Questions about Luke, and questions about her grandfather's estate. As she dressed for breakfast, she ran through yesterday's meeting with Hank Durham, wishing he'd had more answers about Grandpa Henry's affairs.

She had arrived at Durham's office preoccupied with thoughts of Luke. During what had seemed an interminably long drive to Pine Run, Jennifer had found Luke's following behind her in his marked sheriff's vehicle both reassuring and unnerving. Reassuring because he could give her a lift if her car broke down. Unnerving because of the powerful emotions he generated in her, feelings that ran the gamut from anger and hurt to love and desire. With relief, she'd waved him away after pulling in front of the car dealership, hoping she'd have a few hours without emotional turmoil before she'd have to face him again on the ride home.

Durham's office was on the second floor of the building overlooking the courthouse, and reached by a steep set of interior stairs whose treads were scooped with wear. Not surprising, since the plaque on the corner of the building indicated the clapboard structure had been erected in 1903. The stairway opened onto an upstairs hall, with Durham's office on the right behind an opaque glass door with his name and Attorney at Law in gilded letters.

Jennifer entered the reception room, where an attractive blond woman with ringlets massed atop her head pecked at a computer keyboard. A glance at the stack of bridal magazines on the corner of her desk clued Jennifer to the fact that the typist must be Cassie Lou Carwise, the woman rumored to be engaged to Luke.

Jennifer's heart sank at the woman's attractiveness, before she reminded herself she wasn't in competition with Cassie Lou. She had lost that contest years ago.

She scrutinized the paralegal carefully, searching for some imperfection in the blonde's appearance, but found none. No wonder Luke was interested. When Cassie Lou lifted her head and greeted Jennifer, her voice and smile were friendly and seemingly genuine. She ushered Jennifer into Durham's office and closed the door behind them.

Durham, a short, squat man looking nothing like

the rodeo rider she had imagined, except for his craggy, sun-weathered face, came from behind his massive oak desk to shake her hand and wave her into a seat.

When he returned to his own chair, Jennifer noted the wall behind the desk, filled with Durham's law degree, membership certificates for the Rotary Club and Chamber of Commerce, and a graphic painting depicting the massacre at the Little Big Horn, with George Armstrong Custer crouched beneath the standard of the Seventh Cavalry, surrounded by fallen troops and rampaging warriors, pistol drawn in futile self-defense.

"The will is straightforward," Durham said, handing her a copy. "You are the only beneficiary to the trust. Everything is in order."

"Is this all?" she asked, staring at the single sheet of paper in dismay.

His deep brown eyes widened in surprise. "It's over a million bucks after taxes. Isn't that enough?"

Jennifer shook her head. "That's not what I meant. I hadn't spoken with my grandfather in over ten years. I'd hoped he might have left a letter, or some kind of message."

She'd seen movies where the deceased had left a final farewell on video tape, and she'd dared to hope. But Grandpa Henry had never been on the cutting edge of technology, so the lack of such a greeting wasn't a surprise, only another disappointment.

Durham's weatherbeaten face softened. "I'm sorry, Miss Faulkner. If your grandfather left any message, it wasn't with me."

Swallowing her disappointment, she nodded. "Anything else I need to know or do?"

"The estate's pretty much cut and dried," Hank told her. "Your grandfather's farm is paid for, the proceeds from the sale of the hardware store were invested in mutual funds, and the lottery winnings went into the trust."

"What about outstanding debts?" Jennifer asked.

Durham shook his head. "Nothing, aside from funeral expenses, electricity bills and property taxes, which I've already taken care of."

"No one's come forward with a claim?" She couldn't help recalling Finn's words about her grandfather's reaction to his Big Draw prize. What huge debt could Henry have owed that no one seemed to know about?

"I've run the required notice to creditors in the local papers," Durham said. "Even placed one in the Billings paper. That was weeks ago and nobody's responded. I think you can rest assured that your inheritance will remain intact. The only monies anyone could touch would be the proceeds from the farm and the hardware store. The trust is yours alone."

"Even so, I'd like you to place the notice in national papers, like the *Wall Street Journal,* the *New York Times* and *USA TODAY*."

Durham looked puzzled. "That seems unusual, considering your grandfather rarely left Jester, much less traveled outside the county."

Jennifer explained Finn Hollis's conversation with Grandpa Henry and his reference to a huge debt.

Durham rocked slightly in his chair and tapped the tips of his stubby fingers together. Sunshine streamed in the window behind him, revealing his scalp pink beneath his thinning hair. "I'll place the additional ads, but I'm doubtful anything will turn up. Nothing in your grandfather's papers indicated a debt of that magnitude, and Henry Faulkner was meticulous about his record-keeping. He still had all his ledgers from his years in the hardware business."

Jennifer had thanked Durham for his work on the estate and promised to contact him with a forwarding address before leaving Jester. In turn, he'd agreed to call her if there was a response to the nationwide notices to creditors.

"This could get expensive," he warned.

"They're just classified ads. They can't cost much."

He shook his head. "When people get a whiff of easy money, the rats come out of the woodwork. These ads will generate a flood of falsified claims, and every one will have to be investigated and eliminated."

"Wait until I check the farm for paperwork on the debt before placing the ads. Still, I'd rather pay to sort out the frauds," Jennifer insisted, "than to let a major debt of my grandfather's go unpaid. Especially when the money is there to rectify it."

Durham's eyes had lit with admiration. "You're a remarkable woman, Miss Faulkner. Most folks I know would just take the money and run."

She allowed herself a self-deprecating smile. "I'm not saying I don't enjoy the prospect of all that money. But my grandparents taught me that doing what's right is more important than being wealthy."

Durham's face twitched in his own self-effacing grin. "You'd make a lousy lawyer."

As Jennifer was leaving the office, Cassie Lou stopped her. "I'm really sorry about your grandfather. I met him a couple times when he visited the office, and he was a kind and gentle man. I'm sure you miss him very much."

Tears welled in Jennifer's eyes at the woman's sympathetic words and kind tone. Cassie Lou was compassionate as well as gorgeous. No wonder Luke wanted to marry her.

The prospect went through Jennifer's heart like a knife.

That was a wound she might as well get used to, she reminded herself as she descended the stairs to the boardinghouse dining room for breakfast the next morning. Luke McNeil was out of her life for good, and the sooner she was gone from Jester and away from him, the better.

Before she reached the bottom step, she raised her head and sniffed, wondering if Gwen had burned breakfast, because the air was heavy with the stench of smoke.

LUKE ENTERED HIS OFFICE and headed straight for the coffeemaker. He hadn't slept well and wouldn't make it through the day without a heavy fix of caffeine. After he'd left Jennifer at the boardinghouse the night before, he hadn't been able to get her out of his mind. And even when he'd left his car, the subtle fragrance of roses had seemed to follow him, all the way to his bed.

He'd tossed and turned, unable to rest, until he'd finally reached a decision. For his own peace of mind, he'd have to confront her, make her tell him why she'd abandoned him ten years ago without so much as a goodbye. Maybe if he knew the reason— even if he didn't like it—he could close that chapter of his life and move on, without comparing every woman he met to Jennifer and having them all come up short.

He scrubbed his weary eyes with his fists. Lordy, he needed coffee and needed it bad.

Before he could take off his coat, however, the phone on his desk started ringing.

"Sheriff's office," he answered.

"Luke, it's Jimmy." Luke recognized the voice of the custodian at the school. "I've already called in the fire but I wanted to alert you."

About that time, Luke heard the siren wail from atop the fire station on Mega-Bucks Boulevard, next to the town hall—the signal alerting the volunteers of Jester's Fire and Rescue Squad to assemble. Luke thought of the old two-story structure he'd attended for all twelve grades, where every child and teenager in Jester went to school, and his gut wrenched at the prospect of losing a landmark so filled with memories for so many people.

"Is the school burning?" Luke asked.

"Nope, the fire's in the park. I spotted the smoke when I was opening up this morning. Looks like the pavilion."

"Thanks, Jimmy. I'm on my way." Luke hung up, stifled a curse and cast a longing look at the coffeepot before bolting for the door.

He pulled back before exiting, however, to prevent a collision with Sylvia Rutledge, who was pounding the pavement past his office on her way to the fire station. Slim and athletic, the thirty-year-old blond hairdresser, owner of the Crowning Glory, raced past him without a glance, the wind ruffling her already tousled hair, her hazel eyes shining with excitement and determination. Jester's only female firefighter, she'd had to work her butt off to meet the requirements for the fire and rescue squad, and in doing so had won the respect and admiration of everyone in town.

Luke glanced up the street and spotted Dev Devlin a block ahead of Sylvia in his race to the firehouse. From his garage past the town hall, Tex, who served as fire chief, was also hurrying toward the station.

Luke turned back toward the park and nodded as Oggie Lewis thundered past. Oggie appeared scholarly and mild mannered, but when fire or other disasters threatened, there was no better member of the rescue team.

Breaking into a sprint, Luke headed down Main Street toward the town park, where a plume of dark smoke curled into an otherwise cloudless sky. At the boardinghouse, he saw Jennifer with Gwen, Irene and Stella huddled on the wraparound porch, watching the blaze.

He paused at the intersection of Lottery Lane to make certain no traffic was approaching. Behind him, the siren of Jester's only fire truck signaled its approach. He waved Tex through the crossroads, then followed the firefighters on foot.

Across the park, Olivia Mason and Jimmy the janitor were herding youngsters from the basketball courts and baseball field to the schoolyard, out of harm's way and out from underfoot. Behind Luke a crowd was gathering, including the barbershop's usual customers and the early-morning diners at the Brimming Cup.

"Stay back," Luke warned. "Let the rescue squad do its job."

"Anybody hurt?" His brother-in-law, Nathan, appeared at Luke's elbow from the medical center that fronted the park on Lottery Lane.

"Don't know yet," Luke said. "Just got here."

"I'll stand by, just in case," Nathan said.

The fire truck skidded to a halt beside the pavilion wreckage, where flames flicked through the collapsed boards. Dev and Oggie unrolled the hose, while Sylvia, in full firefighting regalia, including a breathing tank strapped on her back, combed the wreckage, perilously close to the dancing flames, searching for anyone who might be injured or trapped.

THREE HOURS LATER, Luke sank onto the front step of the empty and long-deserted Mac's Auto Repair across the street from the pavilion. The acrid taste of scorched lumber filled his throat, and smoke stung his eyes. His body ached from crawling through smoldering wreckage, his energy flagged, and he was ready to kill for a cup of—

"Coffee?" a familiar voice asked.

He glanced up to find Jennifer standing in front of him with a large thermal mug in one hand and a napkin-wrapped pastry in the other.

"What are you, a mind reader?" He accepted the coffee with a grateful smile and took a large gulp of the scalding brew.

"I've been helping Gwen. We've already served the firefighters, but you've kept one step ahead of us. This was the first I could catch up with you."

He wouldn't have thought it possible, but she looked even more beautiful this morning than she had the day before. Her hair shimmered like spun gold in the brilliant sunlight, her aquamarine eyes glowed a deeper sea-blue, and the smudge of soot on her cheek did nothing to mar the flawless beauty of her face. Elegant in designer jeans, boots that appeared to be handcrafted Italian leather and a down-filled denim vest over a turtleneck sweater that matched her eyes, she looked like a model on a location shoot.

He swallowed a bite of Gwen's melt-in-your-mouth pastry and washed it down with more coffee. "I think you just saved my life. I've been in caffeine withdrawal for hours."

Jennifer folded her long legs and settled onto the step beside him, reminding him of too many summer days when they'd sat together on the front steps of Cottonwood Farm. He could feel her eyes studying him, as if searching for answers to some unspoken question.

"You've probably been running on adrenaline," she said with a hint of concern in her voice, "to make up for no coffee."

He must have read her tone wrong. Jennifer Faulkner had no reason to be worried about him. Luke kept his gaze fixed across the road, where

Sylvia and Dev were rewinding the fire hose while Tex and Oggie checked the ruins for hot spots.

Once the initial excitement had worn off, the crowd had dispersed, leaving only the firefighters and Luke to deal with the burning pavilion. The crime scene tape that he had just restrung around the scorched pavilion wreckage fluttered in the southerly breeze.

"Damn," Luke heard Sylvia holler.

Tex looked up from his digging. "Got a problem?"

Sylvia yanked off a glove and wiggled her fingers. "Broke a nail."

"Place up the street can fix that," Tex said in a dry tone. "It's called the Crowning Glory."

"I'm out of luck, then," Sylvia retorted. "Hear the proprietor's been called away on an emergency."

"I saw the mayor here earlier," Jennifer said from beside Luke, craning her neck to search the area, "but looks like he's gone now."

Luke stifled a curse at the mention of His Honor. "He's on my back worse than before to let them clear the wreckage. Says now it's even more unsightly."

"Will you?" she asked.

"Not now." He sipped the coffee, which was kept blessedly hot by the thermal mug. "Not until the structural engineer from Billings checks it out."

"Hasn't the fire destroyed any evidence?"

"Maybe," Luke admitted. "But I want to make damned sure, especially now."

Her eyes widened. "You don't think the fire was set on purpose? Folks were guessing it was a short circuit in the pavilion wiring."

Luke shook his head. "The electricity was shut off after the collapse."

"Was it arson?" Her throaty voice was tinged with disbelief, and he could understand why. Jester wasn't a high crime area. He couldn't remember a case of arson in all his years there.

"Maybe, maybe not."

While his mind wrestled with the problem of the pavilion, his heart reveled in Jennifer's closeness. He had only to shift an inch on the step to slide his thigh against hers, and while he longed for the contact, he resisted the temptation, afraid she would only scoot away. He took delight instead in the easy manner of their conversation, just as it had been all those years ago when he'd loved her so much it hurt.

Hell, who was he kidding? He still loved her, and it still hurt, only the hurt was deeper, sharper now, because she didn't return that love.

Jennifer stared at the smoking ruins. "I thought arson was easy to spot."

"It is, if an accelerant was used."

"Accelerant?"

"A fuel, like gasoline or kerosene, to hasten the spread of the fire. Tex says there's no evidence of that." Luke raked his fingers through his hair in frustration. "Between the fire, the water used to extinguish it, and the destruction of any footprints by the boots of the firefighters, there's little evidence left of anything. All we know for sure is that the fire started underneath the wreckage."

Jennifer looked thoughtful. "That means someone had to crawl under there to set it."

Luke nodded. "Or it could have been kids hiding out to neck or smoke, or a vagrant passing through town looking for a spot to build a fire and keep warm, out of the wind and snow."

Jennifer relaxed beside him. "So it was probably accidental."

"My gut says otherwise."

"Is your gut always right?"

Except where you were concerned, he wanted to say. His instincts had failed him then. He hadn't seen her desertion coming. Hadn't understood it when it came. Sure as hell didn't understand it now.

"Ninety-five percent of the time," he answered instead.

"Why would anyone want to burn the pavilion?" she asked. "It was already ruined."

"To hide the evidence of how it was wrecked."

She placed her hand on his sleeve, and her touch jolted through him like an electrical current. He defied the desire to cover her hand with his own.

"I remember what you taught me," she said,

''about motive, means and opportunity. Who has a reason to want the pavilion destroyed?''

''You've just stated the crux of the problem,'' Luke admitted. ''The pavilion is town property. The structure was insured, so the town receives the insurance money. Those funds, however, will be used to rebuild the pavilion, so nobody really profits. Everything would be just back the way it was before, so what's the point?''

Jennifer narrowed her eyes. ''What if someone doesn't want things back the way they were before?''

Luke drank more coffee, but didn't reply. Bobby Larson and some of the city council members had been pushing for changes in Jester since the Big Draw wins, but did any or all of them want change badly enough to resort to crime to bring those changes about? And what good would burning the pavilion do? Its destruction only created a bigger mess in the park, something that definitely angered the mayor.

''None of this makes sense,'' Luke admitted.

Just like Jennifer's leaving him so long ago. None of that made sense, either. With the two of them alone on the steps of the deserted garage, Luke had his opportunity to ask her why, but his courage failed him. He was dead tired, frustrated over the pavilion and reeking of smoke. He'd had enough bad news for one day. He would wait for a better time.

''Thanks for the coffee.'' He returned the empty mug. ''I'm going back to my office to place a call to the engineer.''

Jennifer stood when he did, and he started to walk away.

''Luke…'' she called to him.

He turned to find her staring at him, her eyes puzzled, her face puckered in a frown, her chin up and shoulders stiff, as if expecting a blow.

''Yes?''

The tension seemed to drain from her, her chin and shoulders relaxed and she shook her head. ''Never mind. And you're welcome for the coffee.''

Ignoring the pull toward her, he turned again and trudged up Main toward his office. If he hadn't known better, he would have sworn she had as many unanswered questions about their breakup as he did.

Chapter Eight

Jennifer watched Luke go, and cursed her own cowardice. She should have asked him the question that had preyed on her mind for a decade.

Why had he abandoned her?

Since her return to Jester, that question had become more perplexing than ever. Over the past years, with often thousands of miles between them, she'd been able to convince herself that the Luke McNeil she'd fallen in love with had been a fantasy, a fictional creation of her teenage mind, fueled by rampaging adolescent hormones. She'd decided that no man could really have been as honorable, trustworthy and dependable as Luke, or as friendly, handsome, romantic and exciting, so she shouldn't have been surprised or disappointed when he'd never written or called. She'd simply made him out to be someone he wasn't.

Being with Luke again, however, seeing him in action, had destroyed the defense of those excuses.

Standing on Gwen's front porch after the pavilion fire was spotted, Jennifer had watched Luke leave his office and rush to the scene. There had been no panic in his movements, no lack of purpose, no wasted energy. He had stopped traffic at the intersection for the fire truck to pass, and had kept the crowd of onlookers out of harm's way.

As impressive as his calm response to the emergency had been, even more impressive were people's reactions to Luke. He hadn't needed to rant or rave to gain their cooperation, just raise his voice loud enough to be heard. The way everyone followed his clear instructions, without questions or grumbling, indicated the widespread respect the sheriff held in the town.

Besides keeping everyone safe, Luke had thoroughly inspected the fire scene, given a hand to the firefighters when needed, roped off the fire area and stayed until the last person had gone.

Maybe he really was as much of a paragon as she remembered.

If so, why hadn't he had the grace to let her down easy ten years ago instead of leaving her twisting in the wind forever, hoping he would call and explain?

Scrubbing away the soot on her check with the back of her hand, she headed back to the boardinghouse. What difference did it make why Luke did anything?

Because you're still in love with him.

Her heart sank at the thought, and she remembered Penny, her devoutly Catholic roommate at
boarding school, who had taught Jennifer that Jude
was the patron saint of lost causes.

Too bad I'm not Catholic, Jennifer thought sadly,
climbing the back stairs to the kitchen door. She
could pray to St. Jude for a miracle. That's what it
would take for Luke to love her again.

Her introspection ended abruptly as she stepped
onto the threshold.

"Wow." She paused in the doorway and surveyed Gwen's kitchen. "Looks like a disaster
area."

Gwen glanced up with a rueful smile from the
table she was clearing. Dirty bowls, baking sheets,
thermal mugs and coffee carafes cluttered the coun-
ters. "Things got a bit hectic once the fire started."

Jennifer shucked off her vest and pushed up her
sleeves. "Let me help."

"I could use a hand. Oggie's showering before
returning to the school, Irene's gone to the bookstore to pick up her new romance novel that just
came in, and Stella's gone to give Sylvia a hand at
the beauty shop."

"Stella's a beautician?"

Gwen shook her head. "No, but she hurried out
saying she could at least do shampoos and sweep
up hair clippings. Sylvia's going to be backed up
with everyone getting ready for tonight."

"Tonight?" Jennifer filled the farmhouse-style sink with hot water and added dish detergent.

"I was going to tell you at breakfast—before the sirens sounded. The historical society is having a dinner and dance at the town hall tonight. Part of the ongoing Founders Day celebrations. You're welcome to come. I plan to take enough potluck for all my guests. But if you'd rather not, I can leave something here for you to warm up."

"Is it formal?" Jennifer swished a coffee carafe in the sudsy water.

"What Grandmother used to call Sunday best," Gwen said. "If you've got a dishy outfit without sleeves or a back, you can get away with it tonight. The weather's warming up like crazy."

A glance out the kitchen window confirmed Gwen's observation. The snow was melting quickly in the hot noonday sun, aided by a warm southerly breeze.

"I suppose the whole town turns out for this, just like they used to?" Jennifer asked.

Nostalgia filled her. Once, years ago, her spring break had coincided with Founders Day, and her grandparents had taken her to the historical society's event. She'd been only fourteen then and had watched with an aching heart while Luke danced with the older girls. Jennifer had almost fainted with surprise when he'd finally appeared in front of her.

"Want to dance, short stuff?"

Feeling awkward and embarrassed by her eager-
ness, she had stepped into his arms for a slow
dance. Even though he'd held her at a respectable
distance, she'd trembled at the contact of her hand
in his, his other planted firmly in the small of her
back, and she'd dreamed impossible dreams. The
dance had ended far too soon, and she'd had to wait
another four years before he'd noticed her again.

"You betcha everyone will be there." Gwen's
reply broke into Jennifer's reminiscences. "It's one
of the big social events of the year." Gwen opened
the stainless steel door of the freezer and placed a
container of fresh-baked pastries, left over from the
morning's distribution, inside.

"You have a date?" Jennifer asked.

She caught sight of Gwen's reddened face before
her friend went back to clearing the table.

"No date," Gwen said. "Not everyone has an
escort."

"Guess there're not that many eligible bachelors
in Jester," Jennifer said, "now that Jack Hartman
and Luke are both taken."

She glanced over her shoulder at Gwen, who kept
her back to the sink where Jennifer was working,
but she could see Gwen's blush darkening the back
of her neck.

"No, not many eligible men in Jester."

Gwen's voice had a strange, strangled sound, as
if she were holding back secrets, but Jennifer didn't
want to pry. If Gwen wanted to share what was

bothering her, she would. Jennifer knew all too well what it felt like to have one's love life go awry. When it happened, you didn't feel like talking about it.

"I'd love to go to the dinner." Jennifer turned the conversation to safer ground. "It may be my last chance to see everyone."

"You're leaving soon?" Gwen whipped around to face her, and the obvious disappointment on her face warmed Jennifer's heart. Knowing someone would miss her felt good.

"I'll be moving out to the farm tomorrow," Jennifer said. "Have to get it in shape to sell. And I won't know how long that will take until I've inspected the place. If there's lots of work, I won't have time to come into town. If there's not, I'll finish up quickly and head for Arizona."

"Why Arizona?" Gwen asked.

"Why not?" she answered lightly, unable to think of a good reason other than it was far away from Jester—and Luke.

"Ever thought of staying here? You have the farm, lottery money to live on and plenty of friends. What more could you want?"

The answer to that question rushed over Jennifer with such a vengeance it almost took her breath away. She wanted to marry Luke McNeil and have his children.

Fat chance. Her grandfather had probably used

up all the family luck winning the lottery. Jennifer might as well wish for the moon.

As enticing as she found the prospect of remaining in Jester, she knew she couldn't endure watching Luke marry Cassie Lou Carwise and raise a family with her. Losing a dream was one thing. Having someone else fulfill that dream while Jennifer looked on was another matter entirely, something she didn't even want to contemplate.

"I don't know what I want," she lied. "I just hope I'll know it when I find it."

The two women resumed their work in companionable silence. In less than an hour, they had returned the kitchen to its usual pristine state. Gwen fixed them sandwiches and coffee, then began preparations for the dishes she would take to the dinner dance that night.

Jennifer went upstairs to her room to change clothes. The temperature had continued to climb, and the roads were clear enough for a run. Running usually emptied her mind, and she needed a clear head to cope with her whirling emotions while she remained in Jester.

After donning sweatshirt, sweatpants and her Reeboks, she limbered up with a few stretching exercises on Gwen's front porch before taking off down Lottery Lane at an easy trot. She hadn't run in several days and knew she should work back into her old stride gradually to avoid injuries, so she stifled her inclination to run like the devil himself was on her tail. Much as she wanted to, she couldn't outrun her problems.

Fortunately, traffic was practically nonexistent in Jester, so she was able to run in the middle of the road, where the snow had melted completely. Weeping banks of slush still covered many of the sidewalks. Her route north on Lottery Lane took her past the library at the corner of Main and by Jester's medical center on her right. At the intersection of Lottery Lane and Orchard Street, she jogged in place, glancing left toward the schoolhouse before taking a right on Orchard Street.

Forging a zigzagging path to avoid puddled water from the snowmelt, she passed the Dupree house on the left. Knowing Shelly was probably working at the diner, Jennifer didn't slow her pace, but continued on toward the next cross street. She turned right on Mega-Bucks Boulevard and stopped in front of the church, hands on her thighs, head bent as she fought for breath.

Exertion hadn't caused her lack of air, but the tightening in her chest when she'd spotted the familiar building where she'd attended hundreds of Sunday services with her grandparents. With a heavy heart, she approached the church, took the path that veered alongside it, and found herself in the cemetery, set on a rolling hill that overlooked the town to the west and the undulating prairie and limestone bluffs to the east.

The details of the day of her grandmother's funeral returned to her in a rush, robbing her of breath once more. Jennifer could feel the oppressive heat of the summer sun, the weight of Grandpa Henry as he'd leaned on her arm, as if afraid he'd collapse if she let go. She recalled vividly the murmured prayers and condolences of the town's folk at the graveside.

Her feet automatically followed the path toward the family plot where Faulkners had been laid to rest for almost a hundred years. Her eyes misted with tears until she could barely read the headstones erected on her grandparents' graves. A stone with her parents' names stood nearby, a memorial only, since the fiery plane crash that killed them had consumed their bodies.

A huge sense of loss welled inside her—grief for her grandparents, a feeling of deprivation for the parents she'd never really had, and the all-consuming, horrible question of why Grandpa Henry had sent her away.

Sent her away? Why mince words? He'd thrown her out.

She was so lost in grief, she didn't hear anything around her, and she jumped in surprise when a voice sounded at her elbow.

"You okay, sunshine?"

"Luke. What are you doing here?" His use of the familiar nickname and her memories of all that it had once meant flooded her with longing and despair.

"It's my business to know what's going on in town," he answered casually, but genuine concern shone in his deep-blue eyes. Time had added tiny crinkles at their corners and etched a fine line between his eyebrows. "I was at the town hall when I spotted you headed for the cemetery. Figured you shouldn't have to come here alone."

She tried without success to stifle the sob rising in her, and when he opened his arms, she didn't hesitate to fly into them.

His embrace enfolded her with a sense of coming home that she hadn't experienced since her return. The warmth of his hard, muscled body eased the chill in her heart, and her tears soaked the front of his suede jacket.

"Go ahead and cry, sunshine," he said gently, smoothing her hair with the palm of his hand. "You're entitled."

She shook her head against the broad expanse of his chest. "I shouldn't—"

"You've lost your entire family. That's a terrible blow." He dug into his pocket, pulled out a clean red bandanna and slid it into her hand.

"I loved them," she sobbed. "And Grandpa Henry…"

"I know," he said soothingly, bundling her closer. "We all miss him."

Standing at the graveside and reading the headstone had brought the finality, the reality of her grandfather's death home. Until now, Jennifer realized, she'd been shielding herself from the truth, pretending that once she reached Cottonwood Farm, he'd be standing on the front porch to greet her, or sitting in the kitchen, smoking his pipe, and glancing up to welcome her with a gentle, loving smile and a self-conscious hug.

Tears flowing, she snuggled deeper into the comfort of Luke's embrace. As long as she had him, she wasn't totally alone.

But she didn't have Luke. Hadn't had Luke for over ten long, agonizing years.

She swallowed her tears and tore herself from his arms, even though pulling away was the last thing she wanted to do. She was making a fool of herself. None of the closeness and passion between them remained. Luke was only being kind.

"I'm okay," she insisted, drying her face on his handkerchief, avoiding his gaze.

"You sure?" Tenderness filled his voice.

For one interminable, horrible moment, she battled the urge to fling herself into his arms again. Her pride saved her. "Yes, thanks."

She longed to say more, but was at a loss for words. She couldn't confront him about his abandonment now, not with her emotions so raw over her grandfather's death. She just couldn't stand any more heartbreak, even if it was ten years old. So she said nothing, standing with her head bowed, unable to face him for fear he'd read the longing in her eyes.

"Maybe you'd rather be alone with your grief."

His words were a statement, not a question, and when she glanced up, he was already moving away.

"Luke?"

He paused and turned, the afternoon sun glimmering around him, giving him a dreamlike quality. "Yes?"

What could she say? *Love me. Don't go. Hold me forever.* None of the above.

"Thank you for your sympathy."

He tipped his fingers to the brim of his Stetson, his eyes hidden by its shadow. "You going to the dance tonight?"

She nodded, afraid she'd cry again if she spoke.

"I'll see you there." He returned to the path and disappeared around the corner of the church.

Her heart jumped with hope at his words, until she remembered that Cassie Lou Carwise would probably be there with him.

Jennifer turned back to the graves, pressed her hands against the cold granite of Grandpa Henry's marble headstone, then traced the letters, *Devoted and loving wife* on Gramma Dolly's, and uttered a fervent silent prayer.

"If you have any pull with the Man Upstairs, Gramma," she begged, "please help me know the right thing to do."

Giving Luke plenty of time for a headstart to wherever he was going, she finally left the cemetery to resume her run, still searching for answers.

A SHORT TIME LATER, Jennifer had finished her run. After leaving the cemetery, she'd completed the circuit of the town, passing the town hall with its familiar statue of Catherine Peterson and her horse Jester, for whom the town was named.

Vickie had dared Jennifer once when she was ten to mount Jester for an imaginary ride. She had accepted the challenge and scrambled aboard, only to be caught by her grandfather, who'd had business at the town hall that day. He'd sent her to bed without supper, but Gramma Dolly had sneaked it into her room that night. Vickie, of course, had escaped unscathed.

The bronze statue had recently been cleaned, but the hall itself looked as if it could stand a new coat of paint, another sign of the town's economic decline.

Beyond the town hall was the fire station. As Jennifer sprinted by, Tex and Dev, out front washing and polishing the truck, waved, and Dev, apparently still with something of the devil in him, cut loose with an appreciative wolf whistle.

Right before the mayor's house, she rounded the corner onto Maple Street and headed west. Crossing Big Draw Drive, she glanced to her right. Behind the Perkins house, Vickie's children played in their fenced backyard. At their screeches of delighted laughter, memories flooded Jennifer.

Memories she'd buried for over ten years, because their recollection tormented her with agonizing homesickness and loneliness.

She recalled a time when she'd been no older than six-year-old Ricky. That hot summer day on this very street, with her bare feet kicking up dust, she, Vickie and Gwen had meandered downtown. With enough change in their pockets to buy a soda and candy bar at Cozy's Drugstore, they'd felt like millionaires. Who'd have thought the three of them would actually be rich one day?

She marveled now at the fact that three small girls had had the run of the town without adult supervision, then smiled as she recalled they'd always had someone watching over them. The entire town of Jester had been like one huge extended family, with neighbors looking out for each other's children as if they were their own. No child—except Dev Devlin—could get away with anything. And none had ever suffered from neglect, either.

Her heart ached with yearning for the feeling of belonging she'd felt then. She really hadn't missed her own parents that much, not when she'd had an entire community of surrogates to fill the void left by their absence.

Across the street from Vickie's was the house where Luke lived. He'd bought the place, Vickie had written her, after Vickie married and his parents decided to sell their farm and move to Orlando. Jennifer couldn't help wondering if Cassie Lou would move there after the wedding, or if she and

Luke would build a new house together. Jennifer pushed that painful prospect aside and increased her pace.

The flood of memories kept pace with her, though, no matter how fast she ran. Skating on the McNeil pond at Christmas, hayrides at Thanksgiving, summer barbecues in the town park. Gramma Dolly tucking her into bed at night. Grandpa Henry sitting by the fire, the big family Bible open in his lap, his index finger tracing the Scriptures as he read.

Home.

But as Thomas Wolfe had so aptly written, according to Miss Van Dyke, Jennifer's boarding school English teacher, you can't go home again. Others in Jester had carried on with their lives, and with her grandparents dead, and Luke marrying someone else, Jennifer felt she no longer belonged, no matter how badly she might wish to stay and make Jester her home.

After turning back onto Lottery Lane, Jennifer approached the boardinghouse, but was loath to return inside to the loneliness of her room. Gwen was probably busy, the other boarders were out and the last thing Jennifer wanted right now was her own company.

Hoping to shake her homesickness, she turned away from Gwen's and headed up Main Street. The stores looked exactly as they had when she'd meandered the street window-shopping as a kid. The old clapboard buildings in pioneer Western style with fake fronts that made them appear taller than they really were remained unchanged, except for their window displays. Signs with the week's specials filled the front glass of the Stop N' Shop Grocery Store, a display of new cosmetics beckoned from Cozy's Drugstore and a selection of thermal blankets and winter jackets were advertised on sale at the Mercantile.

Shifting her gaze away from the sheriff's office as she passed, Jennifer hurried into the Brimming Cup, anxious for a visit with Shelly to cure her loneliness, and equally determined to avoid another encounter with Luke.

Sitting across from Shelly in a booth that overlooked the barbershop and Jester Savings and Loan, Jennifer sipped bottled water and surveyed with dismay the generous bowl of apple crisp with vanilla ice cream that Shelly insisted was on the house.

"I can't eat all that," Jennifer protested.

"Sure you can," Shelly stated. "Besides, you need it. It's comfort food."

Jennifer raised her eyebrows in question.

"I was setting empty crates out back," Shelly explained. "I saw you headed up the hill toward the cemetery."

Jennifer felt tears threatening again at Shelly's kindness, and she dug into the bowl of dessert to stave them off.

"I'm really sorry about your grandfather," her

friend said. "I know how tough it is to lose your family."

"Do you ever get over it?"

Shelly shook her head. "But you have your friends, and eventually you realize that friends are family, and family is everything."

Jennifer nodded. "And now you have a family of your own."

The brilliance of Shelly's smile was blinding. "Who would have thought? I'd figured on spending my days in Jester as an old maid. Now Connor and our baby have changed all that."

"You'll have to send me a birth announcement. And a picture."

Shelly reached across the table and grabbed Jennifer's hand. "Why don't you stay? You have so many friends here. It'll be like the old days."

Jennifer, thinking of Luke, shook her head. "Times—and people—change. Things will never be the way they were."

"That's true," Shelly admitted, withdrawing her hand, "but sometimes things take a turn for the better. I'm walking proof. I was alone, broke and hopeless. Now I'm a millionaire with a wonderful husband and a baby on the way. You've got to have faith, Jenny, that life has good things in store for you."

Jennifer forced a smile. "I'm due for a change in luck, that's for sure."

"Thanks to your grandfather, you're a millionaire, too, now. Maybe your luck has already started to change.''

Afraid to hope, Jennifer shrugged. ''I won't hold my breath.''

Chapter Nine

Loud music and the cacophony of a hundred happy voices rolled over Luke as he entered the spacious basement meeting room of the town hall. The lingering aromas of the favorite potluck dishes of the best cooks in Jester made his stomach rumble with hunger.

Following up on a tip from Dean Kenning, Luke had missed dinner. Even now, folks were shifting linen-covered dining tables against the wall to make room for dancing, and Guy LaRosa's tuxedo-clad band, bused all the way from Billings, was warming up on the stage at the end of the room.

The formal dress of the band was appropriate for the occasion, since the historical society's Founders Day dinner dance was one of the premiere social events in Jester. Not even for this auspicious occasion, however, would Luke submit to the torment of a necktie. With a nod toward propriety, he'd donned a black cashmere turtleneck sweater—an outrageously expensive gift from his sister after her lottery win—a camel-colored sports jacket and dark-brown slacks. Catching a glimpse of Bobby Larson across the room, Luke winced at the mayor's deep purple tux and pleated lavender shirt with rhinestone studs.

In the opposite corner of the room, Dean stood with Finn Hollis. When the barber caught Luke's attention, he raised his eyebrows questioningly. Luke shook his head.

Earlier that afternoon, Dean had hurried into the sheriff's office.

"Remember how you asked me to be on the lookout for suspicious strangers?" the barber had asked.

Luke stuffed the file he'd completed into the cabinet drawer and nodded. "What's up?"

"I was busier than a one-armed paperhanger," Dean said. "Every man in town waited till the last minute for a trim for the dinner tonight. Anyway, this big Expedition pulled up outside the shop and two men climbed out and came inside."

"For a haircut?" Luke checked his watch. He had barely enough time to shower and change before the historical society dinner, and wondered why Dean was bothering him with news of two new customers.

"Nope. Wanted to know if there was a hotel in town."

Luke's ears perked up. Jester was a just-passing-through kind of place. Not many folk actually stayed overnight, not without specific business in the community.

"I told 'em," Dean said, "that the only accommodations were at the boardinghouse, but that it's full up. Suggested they try the hotel in Pine Run. They didn't look too happy about that."

"Did they leave then?"

"Tried to. Finn stopped 'em. 'You got business in Jester?' he asked 'em. 'None that's any of yours,' the bigger of the two told him, real unfriendly like. Then they climbed back in their monster SUV and took off."

"Toward Pine Run?"

"They were headed the other way, but they coulda turned around. I had too many heads to cut to watch 'em long. Gotta get back to work, but wanted to let you know."

Dean took off toward his shop at a good clip for a man his age and size, leaving Luke stewing. In spite of his best efforts to control it, his paranoia kicked back in. Another time of year, strangers passing through might have been tourists or hunters. Even agate collectors off the beaten path. But late March? What were two strangers doing in Jester that they refused to talk about? If they'd had business with someone in town, wouldn't they have asked how to find him?

Unless their business was crime and they didn't want to leave a trail.

For the umpteenth time since that fateful winning day, Luke pondered the mixed blessing the Big Draw had brought to Jester: millions of dollars for twelve lucky winners and the scent of easy money for every con artist and crook in the country. Were the men in the black Expedition ordinary folks with legitimate business or a threat to the people Luke had sworn to protect?

With a sigh of regret—he'd really been looking forward to the best potluck of the year—he grabbed his suede jacket and hat and took to the streets.

Luke had driven around town, hoping to track the strangers down and find out what had brought them to Jester, but the black vehicle and its occupants had disappeared. Too late for dinner, Luke had changed clothes and headed for the town hall.

Once there, he caught the scent of roses before he saw Jennifer, and was glad for the warning. As it was, the sight of her nearly knocked him off his feet.

In the room darkened for dancing, her golden hair with its feathery shoulder-length cut shone like sunshine, a cloud of light above the elegant simplicity of her black wool dress. The long-sleeved garment with its rounded neckline skimmed her body like a blessing, accentuating every delicious curve and ending well above her knees. Her long, coltish legs, clad in sheer black stockings, seemed to go on forever, and the hunger in his stomach shifted deeper in his body. Her only jewelry was a pair of small pearl earrings.

How could any woman manage to look so damned *proper,* so appropriately dressed in mourning for her grandfather, and yet so mouthwateringly sexy at the same time?

"Dean told me where you were," Jennifer said, "so I saved you a plate. It's warming in the oven in the kitchen."

He blinked in surprise at her thoughtfulness, then followed her into the kitchen, unable to take his eyes from the graceful sway of her hips. At the same time he kept reminding himself to cool his jets, that she'd be hitting the road again as soon as Cottonwood Farm was on the market, so there was no point in working himself into a lather, no matter how delectable she looked.

Besides, before he offered body or soul to any woman again, he had to know the reason Jennifer had left him all those years ago. As they passed through the swinging door into the deserted kitchen, he figured the time might have come to pop that unpleasant question.

But Jennifer had questions of her own.

"Did you find them?" she asked.

"Them?" He struggled to regroup his thoughts.

"The strangers in the black Expedition Dean told me about."

He shook his head. "They're long gone. Probably in South Dakota by now."

Her face crumpled in a thoughtful frown. "So you don't think they're a threat to anyone?"

"If I thought that, I wouldn't be here." He'd be sitting in his car on the edge of town, shotgun at the ready, pulling an all-nighter.

His concentration wavered again when Jennifer bent to remove a plate from the oven, giving him an up-close-and-personal view of the black wool pulled taut across her shapely behind.

She turned, set the plate on the table, removed its foil cover and waved him into a seat. The steam rising from the platter made his mouth salivate and his stomach rumble. "That looks good enough to eat."

Jennifer handed him silverware. "It's the best of everything. Shelly's chicken cordon bleu and carrot soufflé, and Olivia Mason's five-cheese lasagna." She removed another dish from the commercial-size refrigerator. "And this is Sylvia's seven-layer salad—a day's ration of vegetables in one dish. For dessert, I stashed away a chunk of Gwen's Black Forest cake."

A thought occurred to him. "Why?"

"It was the best dessert on the table and going fast."

"I meant why did you save all this for me?"

A delightful blush reddened her cheeks. "Everyone else in town was here enjoying themselves. It didn't seem fair for you to go without supper because you're looking out for their welfare."

This was the Jenny he remembered, the woman with the same generous spirit as her grandmother Dolly, the Jenny he'd fallen in love with.

"I appreciate it," he said.

"You're welcome." She poured coffee for both of them and settled into the chair across from him. "Better eat before it gets cold."

He didn't need encouraging. The first mouthful was ecstasy, the others mere bliss. While he ate, he and Jennifer sat in companionable silence, like an old married couple, making Luke recall dreams he'd once had of coming home every evening to Jennifer and sharing the events of their day over supper. What had caused that dream to evaporate like morning mist in strong sunlight? Finishing off the last of the cake, he decided the time had come to ask the question that had rankled him for years.

"Jenny…"

She glanced up from her coffee cup and met his gaze across the table, her magnificent blue eyes full of questions of her own.

Before Luke could continue, the door from the meeting room swung inward and Finn Hollis stood on the threshold, looking dapper and refined in his best Sunday suit, his thick white hair brushed to an elegant sheen.

"There you are, Jenny." He nodded to Luke and looked back to her. "I wanted to claim you for a dance before the band takes their first break. Mind if I steal your date, Luke?"

Jennifer hopped from her chair as if suddenly hit by a cattle prod. ''I don't have a date. And I'll be happy to dance with you, Finn.''

Taking the arm Finn gallantly proffered, she left the kitchen without a backward glance.

Luke swallowed the last of his coffee along with his disappointment. Music filtered through the swinging door, an old tune that reminded him of another dance, almost ten years ago at the Mason farm, the first time he'd ever held Jennifer in his arms.

He'd picked her up earlier at her grandparents's place, where he'd squirmed under Henry's fierce expression, reminding Luke of the promise he'd made the old man about keeping his hands off his granddaughter. When Jennifer entered the room, however, Luke had realized that keeping that vow was going to take every ounce of his self-control. Just the sight of her made him weak in the knees.

She'd piled her long blond hair onto her head, but enchanting ringlets escaped at her ears and the nape of her neck. Designer jeans and a Western-style shirt accentuated her slender curves, and an engaging smile lifted imminently kissable lips. She was happiness personified, and just being in the same room with her made him feel as if he were flying high.

The Masons' barbecue and dance was an informal party, unlike the stuffy historical society's annual affair, and Luke soon found a hay bale in a remote corner of the barnyard, away from the press of party-goers, where he and Jennifer balanced loaded plates on their laps. Foot-tapping tunes from the country-and-western band drifted from the barn, the scents of wildflowers and freshly mown grass perfumed the breeze, and overhead a multitude of stars poked holes in the darkness of a moonless sky.

With her napkin, Jennifer wiped barbecue sauce from her chin, cocked her head and fixed Luke with an inquiring stare. "Don't you like farming?"

Her question out of the blue surprised him. "Why do you ask?"

"When I was little, I assumed you'd take over your parents' farm someday. Just wondered why you decided not to."

"Because I've always wanted to be a lawman."

"Any particular reason?"

At first he thought she was just making small talk, but a closer inspection of her expression revealed genuine interest.

"Ever since I was a little kid," he said, "I've had a respect for laws, for following the rules."

"Don't tell me you never colored outside the lines." Her blue eyes twinkled. Her smile was impish, and he longed to kiss the tantalizing curve of her lips.

Her teasing pleased him, revealing a side to the shy Jennifer that he'd never seen before. "I'm not talking about creativity," he explained. "I'm talking about justice."

"Rules are rules, aren't they?"

Her question was more curious than argumentative, so he gave it serious consideration. "Some rules, like those of artistic conventions, can be broken to good effect, creating new methods of expression. But when laws are broken, people get hurt. That's the difference."

"And you don't like seeing people hurt?"

"No one does, unless he's a sadist or so selfish he doesn't think of anyone but himself. What really torques my jaw is when people behave as if they're above the law, as if the rules apply only to other people, not to them. Those are the kind of folks I want to protect society from."

He flushed with embarrassment at his own intensity. He'd never before spoken so openly of his feelings, but Jennifer had that effect on him. "Guess I sound like a Goody Two-shoes."

"Not at all." Her approving smile reached her eyes and warmed him deep inside. "You sound like Grandpa Henry. He always says the world would be a better place if everybody just followed the Golden Rule."

"Do unto others?"

"It works for Grandpa."

"If everyone was like your grandfather, we wouldn't need sheriffs."

"But everyone isn't like Grandpa. Take Dev Devlin, for instance."

"Dev's not a bad guy."

"But he's always in trouble."

"But there's no malice in Dev," Luke insisted, "just high spirits that get misdirected. He would never hurt anyone. People who don't hesitate to harm others in order to benefit themselves are the ones I worry about."

"The crime rate in this county's pretty low," she said. "Nothing like Connecticut, where I went to school. The headlines there are enough to give you nightmares."

"We don't have the same problems as urban areas," Luke agreed, "and good law enforcement can help create a climate to make sure those kind of problems don't develop here."

She cocked her head and considered him with a seriousness that made her look older than her eighteen years. "Being a deputy where's there no crime—isn't that boring?"

"Good community policing keeps us in touch and interacting with people constantly—"

"You like working closely with others?" Her look of approval was a better reward than a month's pay.

He nodded. "Maybe that's the real reason I didn't want to be a farmer. Just me and the land seemed an awfully lonely prospect."

She gestured toward the barn, where the strains of country music and laughter floated on the evening air. "Farmers aren't always isolated. Neighbors get together to socialize and help each other."

"That's true," he agreed. "But in my line of work, I feel like I'm helping people every day. And that's a good feeling."

He finished off his barbecue and set his plate aside. "What about you?"

"What about me?"

"What do you want to do with your life?"

An appealing blush, evident even in the dim light, colored her cheeks. "I want to think about it. That's why I'm taking a year off before going to college."

"You must have some idea." He studied her as she sat across from him, perched as gracefully on a hay bale as she would be on a designer sofa. With her looks and intelligence, she could be anything she wanted. A model. A doctor. A teacher. A wife.

His wife.

It wasn't the first time that idea had crossed his mind, and its appeal was growing with every minute he spent with her.

"I have an idea, all right," she admitted, her shyness returning, "but it isn't exactly politically correct."

"Now you really have my interest." He couldn't help grinning. "You don't have secret ambitions of becoming a stripper?"

Her startled laughter rippled across the yard like pennies dropped in a fountain. "Why would you say that?"

"It's the only politically incorrect occupation for a woman I can think of on short notice."

"Not only politically incorrect, but lethal, too," Jennifer said.

His imagination kicked in, and the picture almost made his heart stop. "I know what you mean."

"My grandparents would die of embarrassment."

Luke reined in the provocative image of Jennifer in high heels and little else. "Seriously, what kind of career did you have in mind?"

"Promise you won't laugh."

Now she really had his curiosity piqued. "I promise."

"I want to be a mother and a homemaker. Not very exciting, is it? Not like being an astronaut or a Nobel prize-winning scientist."

His admiration of her jumped several notches. "Maybe not as exciting, but certainly more important."

She cast him a wary glance. "You really think so?"

"Good parenting and happy homes do more to prevent crime than all the sheriff departments in this country put together."

His answer was general, but his thoughts were specific. He pictured the home the two of them would build together, the children they would have—an interesting mix of her blond beauty and his dark coloring—

"Luke?"

Her voice broke his reverie. "Hmm?"

"The band sounds really great."

He could take a hint. "Want to dance?"

"I thought you'd never ask."

He set aside their plates and took her hand. When they reached the barn, folks stood shoulder to shoulder in rows for a line dance.

"Uh-oh," Luke heard Jennifer murmur under her breath.

"What's wrong?"

"Line dancing wasn't part of the curriculum at my school in Connecticut."

"It's easy," he assured her. "Want to give it a try?"

A panicked look washed across her face before she squared her shoulders and threw him a brave smile. "Sure. Why not?"

For the next few minutes, they laughed together as Jennifer's feet tangled, trying to imitate the intricate steps, and only Luke's quick grasp kept her from falling. But she caught on—quicker than Luke had, he admitted to himself, when Vickie had tried to teach him—and soon Jennifer was dancing like a pro.

When the dance ended, her cheeks were flushed from exertion, but her eyes gleamed with triumph. "That was fun."

Anything would be fun with you, he thought.

The band shifted to a slow tune, and he grabbed

her hand and tugged her into his arms. She came willingly, easily, as if they'd come together a thousand times before.

He pulled her closer, and the seductive curves of her body melded to his, as if they were part of the same whole, broken apart in the distant past and only now reunited. Luke felt the strong stirring of desire, and only the remembrance of his promise to Henry kept his physical reaction under control, a response Jennifer surely would have noted, as tightly as he held her.

To lessen the tension building between them, he eased his grip so he could gaze into her eyes. "Why does motherhood and homemaking appeal to you?"

She wrinkled her brow in a slight frown, as if wondering if he were mocking her.

"I'm serious," he said. "Why not some fancy career? You have the brains and the opportunity for education."

"Why settle for less, you mean?" He could feel her bristling in his arms.

"Not less," he said emphatically. "I've already told you I think parenting is the most important job there is."

Apparently convinced of his sincerity, she relaxed. "Gramma Dolly made me a believer. She's the happiest person I know, even if she's just puttering around the kitchen or weeding her garden. She gets the greatest pleasure out of the simple things in life—a freshly washed sheet, a tomato she grew herself, a polished floor. And most of all, she loves making a home for Grandpa. She lights up like a Christmas tree whenever he's around.''

''And the motherhood bit?''

''I've always loved children,'' Jennifer admitted.

''That's because you don't have younger brothers or sisters,'' he said with a wry smile.

She cocked her head and the twinkling mischief reappeared in her eyes. ''You aren't casting aspersions on my good friend Vickie, by any chance?''

''Who, me?'' He pretended innocence. ''Why, I just loved when she howled twenty-four-seven the first six weeks of her life. And as for eau de dirty diapers, there's no other stink in the world like it.''

Jennifer's puckered frown returned. ''You don't like children?''

''I'm sure if they were my own children I'd think them the most precious beings on earth.'' He pictured a pudgy toddler—a girl with plump cheeks, eyes the aquamarine of a tropical sea and hair the color of sunshine—racing toward him with outstretched arms, calling ''Daddy, Daddy,'' and a yearning, as strong as the physical pull he felt toward Jennifer, welled up inside him.

He tugged her close again until her cheek rested on his chest, his chin on the glorious gold of her hair. He wanted this woman. In his bed. In his life. He wanted her to be the mother of his children. And he knew exactly what kind of children they would be, because he'd watched their mother grow up in front of his very eyes.

"So you don't think I'm silly?" Jennifer asked, her breath warm on his throat.

"Sunshine, when I think of you, silly is the last thing that comes to mind."

He hadn't let her out of his embrace for the rest of that night. Now, ten years later, remembering, he felt his arms ache for her. He placed his dirty dishes in the sink, pushed through the swinging door and went in search of her. If only for one more time, he wanted to hold Jennifer in his arms again.

JENNIFER SAT on the sidelines with Finn and Dean while the band took a break. Relaxed and happy, she felt the most at home she had since before her grandmother died. If she closed her eyes, she could almost imagine her grandparents sitting at the dance with her, just as they had the year she was fourteen. Everything about Jester, every place she visited, every person she met, tugged at her to stay.

And why not? an inner voice demanded.

Two words, she told herself. *Luke McNeil.*

But Luke had come to the dance alone, something that surprised her.

"Where's Cassie Lou Carwise?" Jennifer asked.

"Who?" Finn said.

"Cassie Lou Carwise is a paralegal in Hank Durham's office," Dean explained. With his lady friend in Pine Run, he apparently kept up with the residents of the county seat more than Finn did.

"If she's from Pine Run, why would she be here?" Finn asked.

Jennifer sighed. "I heard she's engaged to Luke. I thought she'd be his date."

"Engaged to Luke?" Dean laughed, and Finn joined in.

"What's so funny?" Jennifer demanded.

Finn tried to look serious. "The idea of Luke McNeil being engaged. The only thing that man's married to is his job."

"But I heard—"

"Tsk, tsk," Finn said with a shake of his white head. "You should know better than to listen to gossip in this town. Ninety-nine times out of a hundred, it'll steer you wrong."

Jennifer stifled a grin. Finn and Dean were among the worst gossips she knew. Practically every rumor ever started in Jester had its origin in Dean's barbershop. But her affection for the two men she considered like uncles kept her from making a pot-calling-the-kettle-black comparison.

"I saw the bride magazines on her desk." Jennifer tried to squelch her surge of hope that Cassie wasn't engaged to Luke. "She's planning a wedding."

"That young woman's been on the verge of marriage to half the men in Pine Run," Dean said knowingly. "I have it on good authority that any man who takes her out more than three times she considers her fiancé, whether the poor fool knows it or not.''

"Besides,'' Finn added, ''if Luke is engaged to Cassie Lou, why's he headed this way, looking like a cat after cream?''

Jennifer glanced toward the kitchen, and, sure enough, Luke was striding across the floor toward her, his walk sleek and purposeful, but not like a housecat. More like a panther or a mountain lion, with easy grace in the movement of every muscle. When her gaze met his, the tiniest hint of a smile played across his face.

Her heart stuttered, then pounded in her chest as if trying to escape.

He stopped in front of her. ''Would you like to dance?''

Only then did she realize the band had begun playing again, a slow, sensual waltz. As if mesmerized, she nodded, rose to her feet and stepped into his open arms.

Before Luke could take the first step, Dev Devlin appeared at his elbow.

''Just had a customer come into the bar, Sheriff. He says teenagers are drag racing on the Pine Run highway. Thought you might want to check it out before somebody gets hurt.''

''Thanks, Dev.'' Luke dropped his arms and stepped away from her. If he was disappointed, his stoic expression didn't show it. "I'll take a rain check on that dance, Jennifer."

"Sure, Luke." Her voice was light but her heart was heavy. If she followed through on her plans, she'd never dance with Luke again.

Chapter Ten

The next morning, Jennifer loaded the last bag from the Stop N' Shop into the back of Vickie's car alongside her luggage they'd collected at the boardinghouse, then climbed into the passenger seat.

"All set?" her friend asked. "Looks like you only bought half the store. Sure you don't want to go back for the rest?"

"Most of it is cleaning supplies," Jennifer explained. "I hope a good wash will set the farmhouse right. I'm no expert at painting."

"You could always ask Luke," Vickie suggested. "He's handy with a paintbrush."

Luke, Jennifer thought with a sigh, was good at anything he set his mind to. She still stung with disappointment over their missed dance last night. Although she'd waited until the band played their final song, Luke hadn't returned. And she'd seen no sign of him on Main Street this morning as she'd purchased supplies before catching a ride to Cottonwood Farm with Vickie.

"Luke's too busy preserving truth, justice and the American way to have time for mundane chores." Jennifer kept her voice light, not wanting her friend to suspect her disappointment.

"You're right," Vickie agreed. "My brother works too hard."

"He needs a hobby," Jennifer suggested.

"He needs a wife," Vickie retorted. "Someone who'll make him take care of himself."

"I can't see any woman making Luke do something he doesn't want to do."

"The right woman would." Vickie glanced across at her as the car passed the church and headed northeast out of Jester. "At one time, I thought you were the right woman for him, Jennifer."

"So did I." The words slipped out before she could stop them. "Luke, apparently, had other plans."

Vickie looked as if she wanted to say more, but thankfully didn't. Jennifer didn't like the turn the conversation had taken, and was grateful that it had ended. She gazed out the window at the familiar landscape as they sped down the highway toward the turnoff to Cottonwood Farm ten miles out of town. The sky was a deep, cloudless blue, the morning delightfully warm and springlike, but a glance in the side mirror revealed an ominous line of dark clouds approaching from the west.

They passed the entrance to what had once been the McNeil farm, and myriad memories tugged at Jennifer.

''Do you miss the old place?'' she asked Vickie.

''Sometimes. Especially at holidays and birthdays,'' her friend said, ''but Mom and Dad are well and happy in Orlando. Farming's a hard life. I'm glad it's behind them.''

Within minutes of passing the old McNeil road, they reached the dirt road that led from the highway to Cottonwood Farm. Vickie turned in, and the vehicle bounced over water-filled ruts created by melted snow, frost and neglect. Large patches of snow dotted the fields on either side of the road, and ahead, nestled among the gigantic prize maples that Gramma Dolly had coaxed into growing despite the unforgiving climate, stood the farmhouse. The peeling paint made its two-story facade appear sad and neglected.

Behind the house, past the barn and other outbuildings, the cottonwoods for which the farm was named, and a stand of willows, lined the creek.

Jennifer had known coming home would be hard, but she hadn't been prepared for the sledgehammer blow to her heart caused by the deserted homestead. Fighting the impulse to ask Vickie to turn around and take her away from the dismal spot, she breathed deeply to avoid bursting into tears in front of her friend.

"Pull around back," Jennifer suggested. "We'll unload everything onto the back porch."

The women made several trips from the car to the house, and soon all the bags from the Stop N' Shop as well as Jennifer's belongings were stowed on the porch.

"I can stay and help you unpack. Even help with the cleaning, if you like," Vickie offered. "Nathan's with the kids, so I have the whole morning free."

Jennifer hugged her friend. "You're sweet to volunteer, but I'm guessing you don't get to spend much time with the busy doctor. I'll be fine on my own."

"You're sure?" Vickie's gaze searched her face. "I don't mind staying."

"I know, but, really, I can manage."

Jennifer didn't say that she needed to travel this portion of her sentimental journey on her own, but Vickie must have sensed her feelings. After returning her hug, she climbed back into her car.

"At least you have the phone. Call if you need me." With a cheerful toot of the horn, she circled the barnyard and drove away.

Jennifer watched her go, feeling suddenly lonely and abandoned. The approaching storm and icy bite of the freshening wind did nothing to improve her mood. This time there was no Grandpa Henry to welcome her home, no Gramma Dolly to caution her to wipe her feet before entering the house or to envelop her in a smothering embrace. Reluctant to go inside and face the solitude, Jennifer decided to survey the grounds and outbuildings.

First she circled the house, stopping at the front steps to gaze at the bare branches of the maples. They had been thick with leaves that summer long ago after the Masons' barbecue, when Luke had kissed her for the first time, in their shadow. Years before, Grandpa Henry had hung a swing from one of the branches. Soaring high in that swing had been one of the special delights of Jennifer's childhood, but that thrill had paled into insignificance compared to the sensation she'd experienced when Luke had pulled her into his lap on that swing and kissed her until her bones melted.

Shaking away the memory that made her ache, she continued her inspection of the farmhouse from the outside, noting missing roof shingles and cracked windowpanes.

When she returned to the back of the house, she crossed the yard to the barn and eased open one of the wide double doors. In the dim light, she could make out the stalls, long empty of animals, and the hulking outline of Grandpa's Chevy pickup, the same one he'd driven for years before she left the farm.

Sneezing in the dusty air, she hurried outside. The air had turned even more frigid in just the past few minutes, and if she continued to avoid the house, she was going to freeze to death. Bracing herself to enter the abandoned house, she recalled that she might find papers there that identified the person to whom her grandfather owed his huge debt. Better still, she might find some message left by Grandpa Henry that explained why he'd sent her away.

Halfway across the yard, she stopped, struck by an anomaly in the familiar landscape. Gazing to the northeast, across the fields where Grandpa had planted sugar beets in the fertile soil along the creek, Jennifer spotted a strange black silhouette.

It was moving toward her.

As she watched, she realized the object was a large vehicle on the far side of the field, a monstrous SUV. She recalled the strangers Dean had seen in town yesterday, the men Luke had tried to follow—unsuccessfully, as he'd lost their trail. If these were the same men, what were they doing on Cottonwood Farm?

The vehicle stopped, still too far away for her to tell whether it was a black Expedition, and two men climbed out. The taller one pointed toward the farmhouse, and she wondered if they could see her, hidden in its shadow. The only reason she could view them so clearly at that distance was that they stood on the horizon, backlit by the morning sun.

Fear shivered through her, and although she tried to convince herself she had no reason to be frightened, she couldn't help remembering Luke's worries about criminals who might be after the Main Street Millionaires' money. She was miles from nowhere, alone, with two strange men trespassing on her property.

She sidled around the house again, remaining in the shadows, and climbed the front steps. After retrieving from her jeans' pocket the keys Hank Durham had given her, she unlocked the front door and stepped inside. A blast of cold air, several degrees cooler than the outside temperature, hit her, and she couldn't tell if her teeth were chattering from cold or fear.

With little notice of her surroundings, she headed straight for the phone on the hall table. When she picked up the receiver, she almost whimpered with relief at the sound of a dial tone. Sunlight streaming from the living room windows illuminated a list of telephone numbers, posted in Gramma Dolly's neat handwriting, tacked on the wall above the phone. The top number was the sheriff's office.

Luke answered on the first ring.

"Luke…"

"Jennifer, is that you?"

Just the sound of his voice made her feel safer. She took a deep breath to stop her teeth from rattling. "I'm at the farm. Remember that Expedition you were looking for yesterday? I think it's here."

"At the house?" The alarm in his voice sent her pulses racing again.

"In the northeast field. Two men are walking around out there. I don't know what they're doing."

"Are you alone?"

"I had Vickie drop me off."

She heard a muffled curse before he spoke again. "I'm on my way. Lock the doors and don't let anyone in. Take Henry's rifle from over the mantel and make sure it's loaded. You know how to use it if you need to."

His tone had changed to calm reassurance, quieting her fears.

"Maybe I'm overreacting—"

"I'd rather check out a false alarm than have anything happen to you, sunshine. I'll be there in a few minutes."

The phone clicked, closing the connection. Jennifer exhaled a sigh of relief. Luke was on his way. She had nothing to worry about.

She crossed to the living room window, pulled back the dusty curtain and gazed toward the northeast field. The two men were still there, making sweeping gestures with their arms and occasionally pointing toward the house. Remembering Luke's instructions, Jennifer hastened to the front door, threw the dead bolt, then returned to the living room.

She went to the mantel and took down the Winchester hanging there, noting with dismay the trace of rust on its barrel. Henry O. Faulkner, Grandpa's great-grandfather, had brought the gun to Montana over a hundred years ago when Cottonwood Farm was homesteaded. Jennifer recalled many winter nights in front of the fire when Grandpa had cleaned the rifle diligently and oiled it until the shiny barrel reflected the flickering flames.

"The gun that won the West," he'd proudly claimed for the Winchester, "and it's saved many a Faulkner from wild animals—and a few wild humans."

Jennifer didn't know whether the strangers in the northeast field qualified as "wild humans," but she wasn't taking any chances. Working its lever action, she chambered a bullet in the rifle the way her grandfather had taught her, tucked the gun in the crook of her arm and returned to the window to stand watch until Luke arrived.

LUKE PRESSED the accelerator to the floorboard, coaxing every bit of speed from his vehicle's high-powered engine. He started to turn on the light bar and siren, but decided against it. He didn't want to scare the intruders off before he had a chance to question them.

On the other hand, scaring them off before they had a chance to harm Jennifer would be a good thing. Not that he should be worried about Jennifer. Her grandfather had been a good teacher. Even after Luke's weapons training at the academy, she had remained a better shot than he was.

But she wasn't accustomed to handling a firearm

under pressure. If the men threatened her, would she be able to shoot to defend herself?

Luckily, roads in this part of Montana were straight, flat and built for speed. Within minutes of leaving town, Luke was careening onto the dirt road leading to Cottonwood Farm. With the SUV throwing up a cloud of mud and water behind it, he barreled down the drive and screeched to a halt in front of the house. He jumped from the car.

The front door flew open, and Jennifer raced to meet him.

"They're gone," she said.

"When?"

"Just a few minutes ago."

"Which way?"

"Northeast, over the hill. They could still be there now. I just can't see them."

"Hop in." He couldn't leave her alone while he searched, in case the men doubled back to the farmhouse with mischief in mind. Besides, he was happy for any excuse to have Jennifer with him.

She didn't argue. With the Winchester in one hand, she wrenched open the door with the other. She was fastening her seat belt as he started the engine. If she was frightened, she didn't show it, but either excitement or the rapidly dropping temperatures had reddened her cheeks to a rosy hue.

"You okay?" he asked.

She nodded. "Just curious. Why would a couple

of strangers be so far off the highway on private property?''

''Could be they're lost.'' He steered onto the dirt road that ran alongside the creek, toward the rise in the northeast field where she had last spotted the strangers.

Jennifer shook her head. ''I can't imagine who or what they'd be looking for in the middle of a fallow beet field.''

Luke's SUV crested the rise, but the strange black vehicle was nowhere in sight. Fresh tire tracks, however, were evident in the soil still soggy from melting snow. The ruts led to a road on the other side of the field. Luke followed them out to the main highway, where the residue of mud on the blacktop indicated they'd turned north, away from Cottonwood Farm and Jester.

Luke turned north, too, but after traveling several miles at seventy miles an hour, he still hadn't caught sight of the black vehicle. With a frustrated sigh, he pulled into a side road, turned and headed back toward Cottonwood Farm.

''They obviously didn't hang around,'' Jennifer said. ''They've probably crossed into South Dakota by now.''

''If they were lost, maybe they're trying to make up time in their schedule,'' he said in his most re-assuring tone.

''Or maybe they realized they'd been spotted and were trying to get away.''

At the fear in her voice, he shook his head. "Sorry. My paranoia over the millionaires must be catching."

Jennifer shivered. "Can't remember ever having trespassers at the farm before. And I can't help wondering what they were doing out there."

A sleeting rain had begun to fall and ice was forming on the windshield. Luke frowned at the worsening conditions and turned on the defroster.

"Probably just tourists off the beaten track," he said with an air of confidence, but his gut didn't believe it for a minute.

"Tourists in Jester? In late March? You've got to be kidding."

"Mayor Larson and some of the council are under the delusion that Jester could be a year-round tourist draw. Stranger things have happened." He kept the banter light, but his attention was on the road, which was icing up fast in the slushy downpour. They'd be lucky to reach the farm before ending up in a ditch.

"Like the pavilion collapsing?" she said. "Then catching fire?"

"Wish you hadn't brought that up." He could feel his teeth grinding and the tension building inside him. Between the deteriorating driving conditions, the disappearance of the strangers and his residual resentment over Jennifer's long-ago desertion, his anger was building like magma in a volcano, ready to blow. "I talked with the engineer from Billings.

He said it will be several days before he can make his inspection, and Bobby Larson's still on my case to have the park cleared.''

The wheels lost their traction momentarily on a patch of ice. The SUV slid toward the opposite side of the road, and Luke cursed loudly.

Jennifer gasped in alarm and grabbed the dashboard. ''Looks like we're in for an ice storm.''

Luke maneuvered the steering wheel to keep the vehicle on the road, and scowled through the windshield at the darkening sky. ''According to reports, this storm wasn't due until tonight.''

They rode in silence, and Luke gave every ounce of concentration to his driving. With relief, he turned off the highway at the Cottonwood Farm entrance. Where less than an hour earlier there had been mud and puddles, now thick ice glistened as far as he could see. After several agonizing minutes on the frozen mud road, Luke pulled up in front of the farmhouse porch.

''You'd better gather up your clothes,'' he said, turning off the engine. ''I'll wait, then take you back to Gwen's.''

''Why?''

Her question stoked the anger that he'd managed so far to control.

''Because we don't know what those strangers wanted and this storm promises to be a doozy,'' he answered with all the patience he could muster.

''I'm not ten years old anymore, Luke.'' Her

flare of temper was more enticing than petulant. "In this weather, those men aren't likely to return anytime soon. And as for the storm, I can take care of myself."

"Alone out here without a car?" He realized that he was being overprotective, but he couldn't help himself. "And what if the power goes out?"

"There's a woodstove in the kitchen and fireplaces in the other rooms. I noticed earlier that Grandpa left plenty of firewood stacked on the back porch."

"And if the phone goes out?"

"Why would I need a phone? I have groceries, water, heat. What more could I want?" She climbed from the car and would have slipped on the icy driveway if she hadn't grabbed the door handle.

He raised his eyebrows. "A paramedic to set your broken bones? I think you just proved my point. It's dangerous here alone."

"I've been alone for the past ten years." Anger flashed in her eyes. "Why worry about me now?"

She whirled on her heel, an amazing pirouette with the ground frozen underfoot, and stalked up the walk toward the front door, slipping twice, but somehow managing to remain upright and maintain her dignity.

With his own temper blazing, fueled by the anger and blame in her voice, Luke released his seat belt, jumped cautiously from the car and followed her up the icy steps to the front door. She was fumbling with the key and had the door open before he reached her. He followed her inside.

"When did you get to be so danged stubborn?" he demanded.

She placed the Winchester and the keys on the hall table, flipped on the hall lights and turned to face him, her cheeks fiery, her eyes wide with outrage. "None of your business."

Before he could stop himself, he reached for her and grabbed her by the shoulders. "Then listen good, sunshine, because this *is* my business. Why did you walk out on me ten years ago, with no goodbye, no explanation, no nothing?"

Her mouth gaped in surprise before she snapped it shut and shook her head.

"You might as well tell me." He kicked the front door shut to block the frigid wind howling in behind him. "Because I'm not leaving until you do."

Chapter Eleven

The warm, familiar pressure of his hands on her shoulders made Jennifer want to wrap her arms around his waist and lay her head on his chest, but the hard slap of his words sent her wrenching away in anger instead.

"I gave you an explanation," she protested. "You're the one who never responded."

Confusion replaced the fury in Luke's deep blue eyes. "What the hell are you talking about?"

"I left you a letter."

"Oh, no you didn't." Luke shook his head, anger suffusing his face with a fiery glow. "I specifically asked Henry if you'd left me a message. He said you hadn't."

Stunned by his accusation, Jennifer sank onto the bottom step of the staircase that led to the second floor. She remembered vividly the two pages, hastily scribbled while her hand trembled from the shock of her grandfather's rejection and her tears blurred the ink. ''That's not true.''

Luke crossed his arms over his chest and considered her with raised eyebrows and narrowed eyes. ''You calling Henry Faulkner a liar?''

The wind howled around the corner of the house, rattling the windows, and the cold settled deep inside her until her heart felt like a lump of ice. She shook her head. ''Grandpa never lied. There must be some other explanation.''

Luke's skeptical expression didn't change. ''Like what?''

''He forgot?''

''Even when I asked him?''

Recalling the emotional turmoil of the day she'd left the farm brought tears to her eyes. ''He'd just buried Gramma and banished me from the house. He wasn't in his right mind.''

''If there was such a letter,'' Luke said in a voice laced with bitterness and disbelief, ''wouldn't Henry have run across it eventually and given it to me?''

Hurt fueled her anger. ''You're willing to believe I'd tell a lie, but my grandfather wouldn't?''

Luke ignored her question and shivered in the frigid air of the unheated house, which was becoming colder by the minute. ''We're not going to settle this now or we'll freeze to death. Get your clothes. We should head back to town before the weather gets worse.''

She wasn't going anywhere with a man who doubted her truthfulness. She pushed herself to her feet, marched to the wall thermostat and switched on the electric central heat. When she turned back to Luke, she tilted her chin in defiance. "I'm not leaving, but there's no reason for you to stay."

The stubborn set of his jaw told her she was in for a fight. "I'm not leaving without—"

A deafening boom shook the floor of the house, as if a bomb had dropped in the front yard. Jennifer grabbed the post at the foot of the staircase in alarm.

Before the noise had stopped echoing through the house, Luke whirled on his heel, jerked open the front door—and froze.

"What was that?" Jennifer asked.

"You'd better come see for yourself," he answered in a strange tone.

She sidled past him onto the front porch and felt her mouth drop open in astonishment and despair. One of Gramma's magnificent giant maples, its bare branches thickly coated with ice, had been uprooted by weight and wind and crashed down across Luke's SUV, collapsing the roof and buckling the doors.

Luke eased down the icy steps and skidded along the front walk. He tried in vain to open each of the doors and the rear hatch, but the bulk of the tree and the collapsed chassis prevented any access to the interior of the vehicle.

The wind-driven ice stung Jennifer's face. She'd never been so cold in her life. Added to the already unbearable pain in her heart over Luke's accusations was the destruction of the maple that had been part of her life, a treasured memory of her childhood and grandmother. Jennifer's misery was unbearable.

Luke looked as miserable as she felt.

Then it hit her. She had no car. Luke's was undrivable.

They were stranded.

Alone.

Together.

For God-only-knew how long, until the storm ended and the ice cleared.

What at one time might have seemed a romantic fantasy-come-true loomed before her like a nightmare, with both of them mad as hornets and stuck with each other.

"Looks like you'll be staying here, too," she said, struggling to keep her misgivings from surfacing in her voice, and to sound hospitable instead. "You might as well come inside before you turn to ice. That car's going nowhere."

She stepped into the hallway, grateful for the puff of warm air blowing from the heating vent and the welcoming glow from the hall lights.

Luke followed her and had to place his full weight against the door to close it against the increasingly powerful wind.

"Can I use your phone to call Pine Run?" he said. "With me stuck here and my radio inaccessible on the front seat of the car, I'll need a deputy assigned to Jester until this storm's passed."

"Help yourself." Jennifer gestured toward the phone and turned toward the living room. She stopped short at Luke's curse behind her.

"It's dead." He replaced the useless receiver in its cradle. "Ice must have downed the lines."

"At least we still have electricity."

No sooner had the words left her mouth than the lights in the hall went out, plunging the interior of the house into darkness. She could barely make out Luke in the feeble gray light seeping from the living room windows into the hall.

"Gramma always kept Coleman lanterns in the pantry," Jennifer said. "Candles, too."

She brushed past him, all too aware of the citrusy fragrance of his aftershave, his distinctive male scent and the palpable frustration emanating from him in waves, and headed for the back of the house.

"I'll build a fire in the kitchen stove," Luke said, close on her heels. "Good thing Dolly and Henry were sentimental about that old thing and didn't throw it out when they bought their first electric range."

Jennifer was too preoccupied finding her way in the darkness to deal with the nostalgia of her homecoming, but she found herself listening, half expecting to hear Gramma's bubbly soprano or

Grandpa's deep bass calling to her from another part of the house. The only sounds, however, were her own footsteps and the comforting tread of Luke's boots behind her. She hadn't lied about being able to take care of herself and not minding being alone, but she had to admit that, with the fierceness of the storm, the emptiness of the house and the sad circumstances of her return, she was glad even for Luke's prickly company.

Even if he had called her a liar.

Then the full implications of his words hit her.

Luke had never received her letter.

No wonder she'd never heard from him. He believed she'd deserted him without a word of goodbye or explanation. Her heart stuttered at the possibility that he had really loved her, after all. Then despair flooded her again. With Grandpa dead and unable to support her claim, how could she ever convince Luke that she really had tried to contact him? And if he'd really loved her, would he ever forgive her for deserting him without a word?

She stumbled in the darkness and told herself she'd better pay attention to providing light and heat for the house before worrying about shedding any light on her dilemma.

When she crossed the threshold, gray daylight flowed into the kitchen from windows on two sides, and she could see more clearly than in the impenetrable darkness of the hall. The achingly familiar room seemed smaller than she remembered as she crossed to the pantry near the back door. Feeling her way in the closet's blackness, she clamped her hands around the globe of a lantern on the bottom left-hand shelf, just where Gramma had always kept it.

Jennifer picked up the lantern and was grateful to hear fuel sloshing in its base. After carrying the lamp to the round oak kitchen table, she turned to the shelf beside the woodstove. The container of kitchen matches stood in its usual spot, giving her an eerie sense of never having been gone a day, much less a decade. She grabbed a match and prepared to strike it, and was surprised to find her hands shaking so hard from the cold she couldn't make them do her bidding.

Luke stepped in from the back porch, dumped a load of wood beside the stove and took the match and box from her frozen fingers. "I'll do that."

She didn't protest. The cold had seeped so deeply into her bones, that they ached, and she couldn't stop trembling.

Luke pumped up the pressure in the lantern, struck the match and touched the flame to the wick. A warm glow illuminated a small circle around them.

"Maybe we should light another one, too," she suggested.

Luke shook his head. "Better save it. We don't know how long the power outage will last. Are there candles?"

"In the pantry."

He picked up the lantern and motioned her toward the door. "You find them. I'll light the way."

Within a few minutes, Jennifer had located candles and holders and placed lighted tapers around the kitchen to chase away the gloom.

Luke made another trip to the back porch and began lugging in bags of groceries. No one ever had to ask Luke to help. When he saw a job that needed doing, he always tackled it on his own, without coercion and without expecting thanks or recognition.

He paused at the door with bags in his arms. "You okay?"

She shook herself out of her reverie. "I was just remembering the time Grandpa broke his wrist and you showed up every morning before dawn to do his chores and drive him to work before going to your summer job. You must have done that for two whole months."

His grin made her insides flip-flop. "Yeah, you couldn't have been more than eleven. I remember you tagging along. I thought you were a real pest."

"Pest? I was trying to help."

"You were more in the way than helpful, as I recall. It wasn't until seven years later that I found your company so…" His eyes had lost their condemnation and warmed with memory.

"So…?" she prodded.

He hefted the bags onto the counter by the sink. "What's in here? Bricks?"

She shook her head, amused at how deftly he'd sidestepped the memories. "Besides cleaning supplies and some food, it's mostly bottled water. I wasn't sure I could make the pump work."

Luke pulled two of the gallon jugs from a sack and set them in the sink. "Good thing we have these. The well's useless without electricity to operate the pump. At least we don't have to worry about the pipes freezing. Jack Hartman helped me winterize the place after Henry died."

"Winterize?"

"We drained all the pipes so they wouldn't freeze and burst with the house unheated."

Jennifer picked up a candle and checked the pantry. "There're ten more gallon jugs of water in here. It may not be fresh, but it'll do for washing up."

Luke raised his head from lighting the kindling in the woodstove, and considered her with narrowed eyes. "Come over here," he ordered.

Her glance was wary. "Why?"

"Because you're freezing to death."

She couldn't argue with his assessment. The room was so cold she could see his breath fog the air as he spoke. But the last place she wanted to be was closer to the man who'd called her a liar. Apparently his trust in her had evaporated along with his love. The frosty misery in her bones, however, quickly won out over her pride, and she inched closer to the stove, which was already disseminating warmth into the kitchen.

Luke closed the door to the hallway, trapping the warmth and creating a cozy intimacy in the room. "We need something hot to warm us up."

Her face colored at his words, which had brought to mind a scenario as hot as any she could imagine. Too many times she'd longed for, dreamed of making torrid love with Luke. Too many times she'd regretted his promise to her grandfather not to have sex with her. But Luke McNeil was nothing if not a man of his word. He'd never weakened, in spite of her best efforts to seduce him. She'd always regretted that she hadn't succeeded. If she had persuaded him to succumb, at least she'd have had those memories to keep her warm.

She shook away the tantalizing thoughts and reached into one of the bags on the counter. "I'll make coffee. And heat some clam chowder."

With the woodstove pumping welcome heat into the kitchen, she stripped off her jacket and pushed up her sleeves. Luke shucked his jacket, too, and draped it over one if the chairs at the table.

As Jennifer prepared their food, everything she touched in the kitchen inundated her in a wave of sorrow at all she'd lost. She filled the large enamel coffeepot her grandmother had always kept simmering on the stove. Jennifer had found the overcooked brew undrinkable, but her grandfather had loved his coffee that way, the thicker and stronger the better. She sighed. Grandpa Henry would never again sit at the oak table with his big, gnarled hands around his favorite coffee mug.

She was reaching for a saucepan for the clam chowder when she caught sight of her grandmother's apron on the peg by the back door, exactly as it had been the day Dolly had died. With her throat clogged with tears, Jennifer reached for the apron and held it to her face. Through the musty scent of the aging fabric came the tiniest hint of lavender from the sachets her grandmother had kept in all her drawers and closets.

Every hug Gramma Dolly had ever given her had smelled of lavender.

Grief crashed down on Jennifer like the maple that had destroyed Luke's car. Driven from the house by her grandfather, she'd never had time to mourn for Dolly. Now Henry, too, was gone, and the anguish she'd been running from for the last ten years caught up with her with a vengeance.

In spite of her best efforts, a sob escaped her lips and she buried her face in her grandmother's apron, soaking it with her tears.

She should never have returned to Jester. She could never escape the past here—neither her grief over her grandparents nor the fact that she was still hopelessly in love with Luke.

Chapter Twelve

At the sound of Jennifer's crying, Luke glanced up from the oak table he'd been cleaning. The sight of her slumped and quivering shoulders and her face hidden in her grandmother's apron temporarily dissipated his anger at Jennifer's desertion long ago and his current frustration over his ruined car.

She'd lost the only real family she'd ever had, and returning to their lonely, neglected home had to be tough. He'd never lived here, but being in the deserted house made him sadder than he wanted to admit.

Jennifer's tears stirred his compassion, and without thinking of the consequences, he went to her and gathered her in his arms, cradling her against his chest. Sobs racked her body, and he pulled her closer, hoping to ease her pain. She wrapped her arms around his waist, and he buried his face in her hair, breathing in the faint scent of roses.

"I'm s-sorry," she managed to stammer through her hiccups and tears. "I—"

"Shhh. You don't have to apologize to me, sunshine. I miss them, too."

She lifted her tearstained face, beautiful even in distress. "Oh, Luke, why do you have to be so...so—"

"So what?"

"So understanding." She pressed her face against his shirt and cried harder. "Nobody's ever understood me as well as you do."

Her compliment pleased him, suffusing him with a warmth that had nothing to do with the heat radiating from the woodstove.

How could he not understand the woman he'd always considered the other half of himself?

He bent and scooped her into his arms, then settled into Henry's rocker by the stove with Jennifer on his lap. She slid her arms around his neck and nestled her head into the hollow of his throat. His arms tightened reflexively around her.

This time, he wouldn't let her go.

He'd been waiting for this moment, he realized, longing for it for over a decade. With gentle fingers, he tilted her chin until her face angled toward his.

"God knows, I've missed you, Jenny."

Her extraordinary eyes widened in surprise, and her crying eased. "I thought you didn't care."

"I thought you'd deserted me."

"I wrote to you. I don't know why Grandpa didn't tell you."

His head warned him not to believe her, that she'd break his heart again, but the rest of him was reveling in the delicious weight of her upon his thighs, the silkiness of her skin, and the steady tattoo of her pulse beneath his fingertips as he caressed the slender column of her throat.

He lowered his lips to hers, tasting first the salt of her tears, then the honeyed sweetness of her mouth. She twisted toward him, and the exquisite pressure of her small, firm breasts against his chest sent desire spiking through him like a sword thrust.

Go ahead, make love to her. Then you'll feel even worse when she leaves you. Again.

She had sworn she hadn't run out on him, he insisted to himself. That she'd left him a letter.

But she didn't tell you what the letter said, did she, cowboy? How do you know—if such a letter ever existed—that it wasn't just goodbye, good riddance?

He was saved from his raging inner battle by the sudden sizzle of liquid on the woodstove burner and the acrid stench of burning coffee where the pot had boiled over.

Jennifer jumped from his lap and, using her grandmother's apron as a potholder, yanked the pot off the stove and set it on the sandstone countertop.

"Guess the coffee's ready," she said, obviously flustered by his kiss and revealing a trace of the shyness he remembered from when she was a little girl.

Her appealing blush made him yearn to tug her into his arms again, but she quickly turned away to remove mugs from a nearby cupboard. She filled them with coffee and handed one to him.

As much as he wanted to kiss her again, he was grateful for the steaming brew. Even though the stove was pumping out heat, the kitchen remained uncomfortably cool.

"Could you dig a can of clam chowder out of one of those bags?" she asked. "I'll find the can opener."

Tamping down his desire, Luke turned to the bags on the counter and began rummaging through the contents. Looking for the soup, he removed bottles of disinfectant, bleach, cleaning sprays and powders, toilet paper, paper towels—

And one box of a dozen condoms.

Suspicion surged through him. She'd almost duped him again with her demure, little-girl shyness. Hadn't he learned by now he couldn't trust her?

Holding up the box, he regarded her with raised eyebrows, his voice cold. "Expecting company?"

She eyed him with a puzzled look. "What's that?"

With a flick of his wrist, he tossed the box across the room. Caught by surprise, she fumbled the carton and almost dropped it. After she'd turned it right side up to read the label, her face turned a deep crimson.

"Where did these come from?" she asked.

Luke had to give her credit. The woman was really talented at play-acting. He found himself almost believing she was as befuddled as she sounded.

"From the printing on the price sticker," he said, irony dripping from every word, "I'd guess Cozy's Drugstore."

Her puzzled expression remained. "But I haven't been to Cozy's. I only stopped at the grocery."

"And somehow, mysteriously, miraculously, a box of condoms jumped all the way from Cozy's into your bag of groceries?" He shook his head in disgust. "How gullible do you think I am?"

Jennifer's disoriented demeanor didn't falter. "But I—"

"Hey." He raised his hands in a gesture of surrender. "You don't need to explain. You're under no obligation to me. Lord knows, I found that out the hard way ten years ago. If you're expecting someone, I'll clear out as soon as the storm ends."

"Don't be ridiculous." Anger had replaced her confusion. "First of all, I'm not expecting anyone. I have no idea how those condoms ended up with my groceries. Maybe they belonged to another shopper and the bag boy placed them with my purchases by mistake."

The longer she talked, the more evident her anger

became. She slammed the box on the counter and placed her fists on her hips. "Besides, I don't owe you an explanation. It's none of your business."

Was this fire-spitting hellcat the same docile, tearful woman he'd held in his arms just a few minutes earlier? The woman he'd wanted to make love to? What had he been thinking? Although he had to admit she was even more gorgeous and desirable when she'd worked up a head of steam.

Marooned by the storm, however, they were stuck with each other, and making peace promised an easier time for both of them.

"You're right," Luke agreed, trying to sound reasonable. "It's none of my business."

"And another thing," she continued hotly, apparently unmollified by his concession, "you can't hike back to town through all that ice. You'd fall and break your neck before you reached the highway."

"And would you care?" he retorted.

Her anger appeared to dissolve before his eyes.

"More than you know," she admitted in a soft voice that set his nerve endings singing.

Now Luke was the one confused. Just when he thought he'd finally figured out exactly where Jennifer was coming from, she'd thrown him a curve. He turned back to the unemptied bags to hide his bewilderment. "I'll find the soup."

As they prepared lunch together, they worked in silence, Jennifer heating chowder on the woodstove and setting the table, Luke preparing a salad with romaine and tomatoes from the Stop N' Shop supplies. They moved in an easy, companionable rhythm, as if this were a meal they had choreographed before and then repeated a thousand times.

This is what it would have been like, Luke thought, if they'd married the year after Dolly died. Except for the quiet. They'd have a roomful of hungry youngsters anxious to be fed—

"Soup's on." Jennifer's announcement broke into his thoughts.

She placed a plate of crackers on the table and took a chair. Luke sat across from her.

Jennifer glanced up sharply, her expression questioning.

"Something wrong?" he asked.

"I hope you like clam chowder. I forgot to ask."

"If a man's hungry enough, he'll eat anything," he said. Then, at her crestfallen expression, he added quickly, "But I do like chowder."

They both dug into the soup, as satisfying for the warmth it provided as for its flavor. The only sounds in the room were the roar of the wind, the rattle of the windows, an occasional crack of a tree limb breaking under the accumulating ice and the friendly pop and sizzle of the fire in the stove.

Suddenly Jennifer dropped her spoon into her bowl. "Vickie!" she exclaimed loudly.

Luke glanced behind him, half expecting to see his sister, even though he knew she couldn't have navigated to the farm through the storm. He looked back to Jennifer, whose eyes sparked with agitation and whose lips twisted in a sardonic smile.

"Vickie?" he asked. "What about her?"

"Your sister put the condoms in that bag."

"Why would Vickie be carrying around a box of condoms from Cozy's? She gets all the free samples of any medical supplies she needs from Nathan's practice."

"She wasn't carrying them around. While I was shopping in the grocery store, she said she had an errand to run. I'll bet she bought them then."

"For a joke?" Luke was well aware that his sister was an incurable practical joker. He'd been the brunt of her humor on too many occasions. He even had the scars to prove it.

Jennifer shook her head. "Nope. On this issue I think Vickie's so serious she's dangerous."

Luke scratched his head. "I know I'm supposed to be a trained crime solver, but you've lost me."

"Your sister," Jennifer said with a wry expression, "is not only a joker. She's a matchmaker, too."

Luke swallowed another spoonful of chowder and shook his head. "Doesn't make sense. How could Vickie know that you'd be calling me to come out here?"

"She didn't have to know. If Vickie had wanted you here, she'd have found a way to make it happen. You know how she is."

Luke nodded. "She's persistent, that's for sure."

Jennifer set her spoon down again. "You don't think…"

"Think what?"

"No, it's too far-fetched, even for Vickie."

Luke grimaced, but his tone was affectionate. "Nothing's too far-fetched for my sister."

"Would she have hired those men in the Expedition to trespass, knowing I'd probably call you?"

Luke broke a cracker, popped half in his mouth and chewed thoughtfully. "If she'd thought of it. But I think you're giving her matchmaking instinct too much credit."

Jennifer dipped into her chowder again. "Of course, you're right."

Luke pointed to the window and shrugged. "But as for this ice storm and downing a tree on my car, I wouldn't put that past Vickie at all."

THE COLD, HARD KNOT in Jennifer's chest eased as their laughter rang through the kitchen. This was the way she remembered the room—full of warmth, light, delicious aromas and, most of all, happiness.

And being here with Luke, still tingling from his kiss, she felt the happiest she'd been since she'd left Cottonwood Farm all those years ago.

Even as she savored the joy of the moment, however, she reminded herself that her happiness was only temporary. His kiss had been consolation, an expression of sympathy, and nothing more. As soon as the storm passed, Luke would be gone, and Jennifer would be left in the large, lonely house with only memories for company.

She realized now that she could never live at Cottonwood Farm. Even though she'd been a loner the past ten years, she'd always resided in places where she could forget the memories that haunted her. Remaining at the farm would bring her face-to-face every waking minute with the reality of all she'd lost. Her original plan was best. Clean the place up, sell it and move on. Goodbye, Gramma and Grandpa. Goodbye, Jester. Goodbye, Luke.

Goodbye to the only real happiness she'd ever known.

"What's next?" Luke asked, as if he'd read her mind. He'd finished his lunch and was carrying his dishes to the sink.

"Next?"

He deposited his dishes and turned back to her. "Just because there's a storm raging outside doesn't mean we can't work in here. Since I'm stuck, I might as well help. Where do you want to start?"

"I haven't had a chance to inspect the house yet, so I don't know what needs to be done." She set her dishes in the sink, too, but, filled with reluctance at viewing the rest of the house, didn't move.

Luke seemed to sense her distress. "Let's take a survey. If we both carry a lantern, we'll have enough light to assess each room."

His reassurance gave her courage, and she reached for a lamp.

"Better put your coat on," he suggested. "The rest of the house will be freezing."

After they'd bundled into their jackets, Luke led the way into the hall, with Jennifer right behind him.

"Jack Hartman and I cleaned the place up some after Henry passed away," Luke explained. "Shoveled out several bags of trash and years' worth of old newspapers. Your grandfather didn't care what the house looked like after Dolly died."

"Except for the dust and dirt, it looks exactly as I remember it." Jennifer circled the living room, making a mental list: dust and polish furniture, launder draperies, wash windows, clean the carpet and scrub baseboards and woodwork.

She noted similar tasks in the dining room, then followed Luke down the hall toward her grandparents' room. Luke stopped in the doorway and placed his hand on her shoulder.

"There's something you should know before you go in here." His voice was gentle, but his words made her heart race.

"What?"

"This is the only room in the house Henry kept clean. He dusted it every day and kept it like a shrine. Except for clearing the dust, nothing's been changed since the day your grandmother died. The room's exactly as Dolly left it."

The image of her grandfather faithfully tending the room brought tears to Jennifer's eyes. "But this was their bedroom. Where did he sleep?"

"He put a cot in his study at the end of the hall. Moved all his clothes there, too."

Jennifer felt as if her heart would break. She should have come home in spite of her grandfather's banishing her. She could have taken care of him, kept him company, eased his loneliness.

And her own.

But his behavior had turned so bizarre after Gramma's death, would he have let Jennifer set foot in the house again, much less have allowed her to stay?

Thrusting away the might-have-beens, she stepped across the threshold into her grandparents' bedroom. It was like stepping back in time.

The big four-poster bed stood where it always had between the two windows on the south wall. The bedspread with its intricate candlewicking embroidery that Gramma had done herself was neatly arranged, although dingy with age.

The dressing table held a picture of her grandparents in a silver frame, the same one Jennifer had taken at their fortieth anniversary celebration. Love sparkled in their eyes as they gazed at one another, captured for all time in the camera's eye. A silver-backed comb and brush set, one that had belonged to Gramma's grandmother, lay beside the picture.

A crystal vase held the dried remains of flowers long dead.

Tucked beneath the edge of the four-poster were Gramma's slippers, as if she'd just stepped out of them, and her fluffy pink velour robe lay draped across the foot of the bed.

"I don't understand," Jennifer said. "Grandpa was the least sentimental person I knew. Gramma always had to remind him, in her gentle, subtle way, of course, about birthdays and anniversaries. Keeping this room as a shrine was totally out of character for him. He was too pragmatic, no-nonsense—"

She feared she was going to cry again, but the firm pressure of Luke's arm around her shoulders helped keep the tears at bay.

"Your grandfather was never himself after Dolly died," Luke said. "It's as if he'd given up on life."

Jennifer swallowed her tears and scooted from beneath Luke's arm, afraid to become too comfortable with his touch. "Let's check the rest of the house."

THE EXTREME COLD of the unheated building grew more bitter with the storm's growing power and the day's waning light, and eventually drove them back to the relative warmth of the kitchen.

After several games of hearts and multiple hands of gin rummy, they dined on grilled cheese sandwiches, apples and chocolate chip cookies.

Through the entire afternoon and into the evening, Luke had wrestled with conflicting impressions of Jennifer. Her obvious distress over returning home and learning of her grandfather's last years disproved Luke's theory that she had turned hard-hearted and cold after leaving Jester. Her love of Cottonwood Farm had been evident in their tour of the house. But he'd also sensed her restlessness, as if she couldn't wait to leave.

She claimed she'd left him a letter, and she appeared to be telling the truth, but he couldn't figure out what had happened to the message—if it had really ever existed.

While Jennifer washed the supper dishes, Luke went upstairs to her old room and wrestled the mattress off her double bed and down the stairs.

"What are you doing?" she demanded when he manhandled the mattress into the kitchen.

"Fixing us a place to sleep. We'd freeze in the bedrooms."

He could almost see the hackles rise on her neck, and there was no mistaking the distress in her voice. "The bedrooms have fireplaces. I'll be fine in my old room. You can sleep in here if you like."

He flashed her an apologetic grin. "You won't be fine in your old room. This is your mattress."

"Then I'll sleep in the guest room." Her voice now held an edge of desperation.

Luke dropped the mattress next to the stove. "It's minus two degrees Fahrenheit outside. Even if you started a fire in the guest room now, it would take hours to warm the room to a bearable level. The kitchen's already warm.''

''But there's only one mattress.''

''Don't try to read something into this that isn't there. Our body heat will keep each other warm during the night. Especially once the fire dies down.'' He tried to convince himself of the practical reasons for their sleeping arrangements, but the thought of lying with Jennifer in his arms generated a quiver of longing deep inside that he couldn't deny.

Spending the afternoon with her had reminded him of all the reasons he had loved her in the first place. It wasn't just her extraordinary beauty that drew him, but her intelligence, her humor, her rejection of the material riches of her parents in favor of the solid, old-fashioned values she'd learned at Cottonwood Farm, and her genuine caring and compassion for her grandparents.

Luke was beginning to believe the inconceivable, that for some twisted, unexplainable reason, Henry actually had sent Jennifer away and broken all contact. As moved as she was by her homecoming, Luke realized, she would have been back long before now if she'd felt she'd have been welcomed.

Her inheritance obviously wasn't a factor. She hadn't mentioned the money or what she planned to do with it. If the fact that she was now a millionaire had registered with Jennifer, it hadn't made much of an impression.

Apparently, however, she didn't share his enthusiasm for keeping each other warm all night. "I'll wrap in a quilt and sleep in the rocker," she insisted.

"Suit yourself." He shrugged, as if her reluctance hadn't affected him, when in reality, all he wanted was to hold her in his arms again.

She disappeared into the hallway and returned with an armload of sheets, pillows and down comforters. "At least the cedar closet kept these fairly fresh. They're not as musty as the rest of the house."

He took the linens from her arms and spread the sheets and one of the comforters on the mattress. The bed looked inviting, but Luke wasn't sleepy. He wondered if he'd be able to rest with Jennifer so close but beyond his reach.

She took the other comforter, flung it around her shoulders and settled in Henry's rocker. Luke fed more wood into the store and sat in Dolly's chair next to Jennifer.

"I've been wondering," he said, trying to find the courage to ask the question that had bugged him since her return. "You always said you wanted a home and children. I figured you'd have been long married by now."

"Never stayed in one place long enough," she

answered quickly, and the pain in her eyes made him wish he hadn't asked.

"That doesn't sound like you. The Jennifer I knew was a homebody, not a rover."

"It's been ten years. I'm not the girl you knew anymore."

"Either that," he said, studying her face in an effort to decipher what was going on behind those gorgeous eyes shuttered with thick lashes, "or I never really knew you in the first place."

"But you did! You knew me better than anybody." Her words came in a rush, and, as if regretting them, she blushed furiously.

Loss welled in him like a geyser ready to blow. "What happened to us, Jennifer?"

"What's that old saying? Circumstances beyond our control?" She shivered and tugged the comforter closer. "You'd better get some sleep. If the storm passes, you'll have your work cut out for you tomorrow."

If she had once loved him, she apparently didn't want to acknowledge those feelings now. And she was right about tomorrow's chores. He'd have to find Henry's chain saw, clear the maple off his SUV and use its battery to jump-start Henry's old pickup, still parked in the barn.

Luke stoked the fire with more wood and extinguished the lanterns. The room plunged into immediate darkness. He sat on the mattress, pulled off his boots and slid between the sheets. But it was a long time, listening to the soft, tantalizing sound of Jennifer's breathing, before he fell asleep.

Chapter Thirteen

The quiet jerked Jennifer out of a sound sleep. Sore and stiff from sleeping in the chair, she stretched and tried to get her bearings in the darkness of her strange surroundings. The silence that had awakened her indicated the storm had passed. The wind wasn't shaking the windows as if trying to force its way inside, and ice no longer pelted the glass.

And the crackle of burning wood had ceased, also. Racked by bone-deep cold that caused her teeth to chatter, she realized she'd have to restart the fire or she and Luke would both freeze.

She flung aside the cumbersome quilt and felt her way through the darkness to the stove. Once she'd opened the door to the firebox, the glow from the dying embers and moonlight streaming in the kitchen windows from the clearing sky cast just enough light for her to find the wood Luke had stacked nearby, and to fill the cavity. With shredded newspapers, she coaxed the embers into flames, and soon the wood caught fire, as well.

By now, however, she was even colder than before. She pivoted on her heel, prepared to rush back to the enveloping warmth of the comforter, when her other foot bumped the edge of the mattress where Luke slept. Unable to catch herself—the only thing at hand was the hot stove—she felt herself pitching forward.

Right on top of Luke.

He awakened with an *"ummphff,"* and his arms closed around her.

"Sorry," she muttered, and attempted to pull away.

His strong embrace held her fast, and in the pale moonlight, she could read the amusement in his eyes.

"We have to quit meeting like this, sunshine." His reference to their previous collision outside the bookstore didn't lessen her embarrassment.

"I tripped." Again she tried to rise, but he wouldn't let her go.

"You're freezing." He released her long enough to tug the covers from under her, then whipped them around both of them. She was now lying along the hard, firm length of him, her lips mere inches from his, his warm breath like a summer breeze against her face.

"I'll…b-be…f-fine…" She couldn't finish her sentence because she shook so hard from the cold.

Or was it the excitement of being so close to Luke again after all those years?

He tugged her closer, and with strong but gentle hands began rubbing her arms, her back, and legs. "You need to get the blood flowing again. You're like a block of ice."

At his touch, fire seemed to course through her veins, alleviating the chill. She propped herself on her elbows to stare down at him. "Are you calling me frigid?"

"If it walks like a duck, quacks like a duck—"

She swatted at him playfully. "As I recall, you were always the one with reservations."

His deep blue eyes turned smoky with desire. "No reservations. Only a promise to your grandfather."

Her body melded to his and throbbed with longing. "But Grandpa's gone, and I'm a big girl now. I can make my own decisions."

She dipped her head and his came up to meet her. With a groan of pleasure, she opened her mouth to his, and he returned her kiss with a fierceness that fired her blood and drove away every remnant of cold, leaving only white-hot heat and desire. She abandoned all conscious thought as he explored the curve of her back, the swell of her breasts, the contours of her thighs.

With gentle but eager hands, he eased the shirt from her shoulders, the jeans from her hips. In the haste of her own excitement, she pulled at his clothes until they were both naked beneath the comforter. Sparks showered along her nerve endings, igniting a tremor of need, making her long for more.

She traced the strong line of his jaw with one finger, and he threaded his own fingers through her hair, pulling back her head to skewer her with a gaze so filled with passion she trembled at the sight of him.

With one powerful movement, he rolled her over and bent above her, trailing kisses from her throat, across her breasts and down the length of her until her body arched in ecstasy beneath him.

"Please, Luke—"

He shoved back, rose from the mattress and moved away. Her heart sank, and her body ached with unfulfilled need. Surely he wasn't still honoring his promise to her grandfather? His withdrawal could mean only one thing.

He didn't want her.

Then suddenly he was beside her again, drawing her against him with one arm, his other hand brandishing the box from Cozy's Drugstore. With a devilish grin, he held it up for her to see.

"Remind me to thank my sister," he said with a delicious laugh. "Now, where were we?"

THE ROAR OF THE CHAIN SAW split the early-morning calm. The storm had passed, leaving the countryside glittering in ice. When the rising sun struck the frozen landscape, it shimmered like prisms reflecting the full spectrum of colors. A breathtaking sight, Luke thought.

And a pain in the butt.

Forcing his attention to the job at hand, he attacked the downed maple with Henry's chain saw again, working his way toward the hood of his car in hopes of extracting the battery. But his mind kept wandering to the night before. Over the years, he'd dreamed many times of making love to Jennifer, but not one of his dreams had come close to the joyful reality. Joining his body with hers had produced not only exquisite physical pleasure, he'd also felt emotionally fulfilled for the first time in his life. She *was* the other half of him that he'd been longing for, the one who made him whole.

Then why the hell hadn't he told her how much he loved her?

Because you're still afraid she's going to leave you again, an inner voice taunted him. *She's never said she's going to stay.*

With a sigh of disgust, he shut down the chain saw. If he kept on while his thoughts whirled, he'd either chop off his fingers or butcher his vehicle. At the slam of the front door, he looked up to see Jennifer standing on the porch, her face contorted with sorrow.

His heart wrenched with pain. Was she already regretting last night? When she awoke with a smile in his arms this morning, he'd had the distinct impression she'd enjoyed their lovemaking as much as he had. And over the breakfast he'd cooked, she'd chattered happily about the day's tasks that lay before them.

Right now, however, she looked as if the world had caved in on her.

He laid the chain saw aside and walked gingerly toward her over the icy terrain. "What's wrong?"

His heart swelled with love. Even with her face stricken with grief, she was the most attractive woman he'd ever seen. Desire stirred within him again, but he tamped it down. In her current state, the last thing she needed was a romp in the hay. She obviously wanted comforting.

"Come inside." Emotion choked her voice. "There's something I want to show you."

He followed her through the chilly house to the warmth of the kitchen. The only thing that had changed in the room since he left it was the addition of a huge Bible, centered on the round oak table. Jennifer laid her hand on it.

"I brought this in from the front room," she explained. "It's been in the family for generations and holds the records of all the Faulkner marriages, births and deaths."

"I can understand why reading those would make you sad."

"That's not what upset me." She flipped open the Bible, removed an envelope and handed it to him. "This is. Read it."

The envelope was addressed to Jennifer in a thin, spidery handwriting. "From Henry?" Luke asked.

Jennifer nodded and sank into the nearest chair. "It explains a lot."

Luke pulled the folded pages from the envelope, spread them open on the table and noted the date on the top page, a few days after the Big Draw win. He began to read:

Dear Jennifer,

If you're reading this, it means I'm dead, but don't be sad for me. I'm with your grandmother now and finally at peace. She was one of God's own saints, so I know she'll forgive me for what I've done. I can only hope that you will, too.

I've been a foolish and stubborn man, and those qualities have kept me from seeing what's most important in life, even when it was staring me in the face. For my entire life, I took for granted that I was married to the most wonderful and loving woman in the world. In the early days of our marriage, we both had to work hard to keep the farm and the hardware business going and to earn enough to pay our bills and set aside enough for your father to finish college. After he married your mother, things were easier for us, and when I retired, Dolly and I were not wealthy, but comfortable.

I should have seen that she was lonely here at the farm, but I was always anxious to spend time with my friends at the barbershop. On days when I should have been with her, I went to town instead, to hang out with "the boys." Don't get me wrong. Your grandmother, God rest her soul, never complained. She was always happy to see me and never said a cross word. But after she died, I realized what I'd lost, what I'd taken for granted, and the guilt nearly drove me crazy.

That's why I sent you away, my darling granddaughter. Old fool that I was, I couldn't stand the sight of you. You look so much like my beloved Dolly that all you did was remind me of my loss—and my guilt. In the depths of my grief and pain, I made you leave.

Later, when I realized what I'd done, I was too proud to admit my mistake and ask you to come home. I guess I was afraid, too, that if I did ask, you would refuse. And I wouldn't blame you after the horrible way I'd treated you.

For years, I wondered how I could make up to you for what I'd done. I'd always planned to leave you Cottonwood Farm, of course, but I know it's not the most prime piece of real estate in the world, even though I love it. That's why, when I won the lottery, I felt as if a weight had lifted from my shoulders. Now

I can at least repay a part of the huge debt I owe you, even if only by guaranteeing your financial security.

I've thought about you every day since you went away, Jennifer dear, and even though I acted like the world's biggest idiot, your old grandfather always loved you. Just like he loved your grandmother, but was too dumb to show it.

Take the money and have a happy life. And when you marry—and I hope you'll find a good man worthy of you—don't ever take him or your life together for granted. Treasure each and every day with each other as God's precious gift.

Forgive me, Jennifer. I love you.

Grandfather Henry

Luke folded the pages and slipped them back into the envelope. "No wonder your grandfather was so depressed. Not only was he grieving for your grandmother, he was also suffering guilt for the way he'd ignored her, and for sending you away."

Jennifer nodded. "That explains the large debt he owed that Finn Hollis told me about, too. But Grandpa was too hard on himself. I don't think Gramma felt all that neglected."

"But if she loved him as much as she seemed to, I know she would have liked more of his time," Luke said.

He thought with regret of all the time with Jennifer that he'd lost because of the old man's guilt, and he swore to himself not to waste another second. He'd wanted to marry her all those years ago. After their lovemaking last night, he was more certain than ever that he wanted to spend his life with her.

"Jennifer—"

A loud banging on the front door interrupted his planned proposal.

"Who do you suppose that is?" Jennifer asked. "Aren't the roads still closed?"

She started for the front of the house, but Luke, remembering the strangers in the black Expedition, pulled her back. "Let me go first, just in case."

She stepped aside, then followed him to the front door. Luke spotted Tim Cates, the deputy who'd helped him during the media blitz after the lottery win, through the glass pane.

Luke opened the door and spotted a sheriff's van with all-terrain tires parked behind his demolished vehicle. "What brings you out here, Tim?"

"Power company linemen have been out since before dawn. One of them spotted your car and radioed the Pine Run office. They sent me out to pick you up and take you back to town."

Luke nodded. "Got room for another passenger?"

"Sure," the deputy said.

"I can stay here—" Jennifer began.

"I wouldn't recommend it, ma'am," Tim said. "If you have a place to stay in town, power's already restored there. Can't guarantee how soon it'll be before you have electricity and phones out here."

Jennifer didn't protest again. "I'll get my things."

Minutes later, they were in the van headed back to Jester. With Luke riding shotgun, and Jennifer in the back seat, he didn't even have a chance to squeeze her hand, much less pop his very important question.

FOUR DAYS LATER, Jennifer sat across from Vickie in her friend's cozy breakfast nook. Warm spring sunlight streamed through the window as they watched the children playing in the backyard.

Vickie took a sip of her coffee and tapped a newspaper folded on the table between them. "Have you seen this?"

Jennifer shook her head. "The *Plain Talker?*"

"Plain talk I could stomach," Vickie said with a grimace. "The column is 'Neighborly Nuggets from Jester.' More like flat-out gossip, I call it."

"What's it say?" Jennifer was glad for anything to take her mind off Luke. She hadn't seen or spoken to him since he and the deputy had dropped her at Gwen's the morning after the storm.

Vickie picked up the paper and began to read. "Rumor has it that Ruby Cade has officially filed for divorce from her husband, Sam. No one in town has laid eyes on Sam Cade since before the Big

Draw win, and everyone's wondering what's happened to the military man. In addition, neighbors are speculating over Ruby's purchase of the old Tanner farm and her plans to work it herself.''

"Who writes this stuff?" Jennifer said.

Vickie shook her head. "No one knows. If they did, half the population would ride the columnist out of town on a rail."

"And the other half?"

Vickie grinned. "They'd watch and applaud."

"You can't take it too seriously," Jennifer said with a shrug. "There're always rumors."

Vickie raised an eyebrow and fixed her with a stare with eyes so much like Luke's, Jennifer found herself thinking of him in spite of her efforts not to.

"You're in here, too, you know," Vickie said in a voice a bit too casual.

"Me? What on earth could anyone find interesting about me?"

"Listen to this. 'What handsome Jester lawman spent the night of the ice storm stranded with which Jester millionaire? Will there be wedding bells in their future? A bundle of joy for Christmas? Stay tuned for more.'" Vickie tossed the paper aside. "Well?"

Jennifer had almost dropped her coffee cup at hearing the rumors. "Definitely no bundle of joy."

Vickie nodded knowingly. "You unpacked the grocery bags and found my little present."

"As for wedding bells," Jennifer said with a shake of her head, "I wish I knew the answer. I haven't even talked to Luke since the storm."

"He's been busy," Vickie explained. "Even though it's not part of his job description, since the storm my brother has visited every outlying farm within twenty miles of Jester."

"Why?"

"He worries that people could be stranded without heat, food or water, especially some of the older folks."

A warm appreciation for the man she loved filled Jennifer. "That sounds like Luke. He really cares about people, doesn't he?"

Vickie cocked her head. "How about one person in particular?"

"Me?" Jennifer shrugged, trying to act as if she didn't care. "The storm's long past. Now that my car's fixed, I'm heading back to the farm today, and I still haven't heard from him."

"You could always give him a call."

Jennifer had thought about contacting him, but what would she say? What if their lovemaking had been only a one-night stand for Luke, a way of keeping warm on a cold night? After all, he hadn't once said he loved her. But then, she hadn't told him she loved him, either.

And she did. So much it hurt.

"But even if you call today," Vickie said, "you probably won't reach him. He's meeting with the structural engineer from Billings about the pavilion."

"How do you know all this?"

"I took supper over last night when he dragged in dead tired around ten o'clock," Vickie said. "Waved his favorite casserole under his nose and swore he wouldn't get a bite unless he told me what he'd been up to."

"Did he mention me?" Jennifer couldn't help asking.

Vickie studied her nails. "As a matter of fact, he did."

"And?"

"And what?"

Vickie's pretense at not understanding made Jennifer want to kick her under the table. "What did he say about me?"

"He asked if I'd seen you, if you were okay."

"And?"

"I said yes and yes."

"And that's it?" Disappointment washed through her.

"The man was exhausted," Vickie explained with a sympathetic expression. "I'm surprised he could even talk at all. If I see him, should I give him a message?"

Jennifer shook her head and pushed herself to her feet. Anything she had to say to Luke would have to be said in person. If she ever saw him again. "Thanks for the coffee."

THE FOLLOWING MORNING, Luke headed his pickup toward Cottonwood Farm. Jennifer's voice on the phone, asking him to please come right away, had sounded strange.

"Are the strangers back?" he'd asked.

"No, this is personal," she'd said. "Please come as soon as you can."

Personal.

He hadn't had time for a personal moment since the morning they'd left Cottonwood Farm with Deputy Cates. Between checking on outlying farms, extricating his sheriff's vehicle from beneath the downed maple and overseeing the engineer's inspection of the pavilion, he hadn't had a moment to himself, except for the brief seconds between falling into bed and falling asleep. At those times, he'd ached to hold Jennifer in his arms again.

He depressed the accelerator, anxious to see her and equally anxious to put as much distance as he could between him and the mayor. Yesterday, the mayor had had a city crew hovering like vultures, waiting for the engineer to complete his survey of the pavilion wreckage so they could cart it away to the landfill. Luke hadn't wanted to hang around this morning while Bobby Larson was politicking in the Brimming Cup, pushing his plans for a hotel built on land in the city park.

Jennifer's call had come as a welcome excuse to get out of town, and most of all, to see her again. He wouldn't hesitate this time. He intended to ask her to marry him and stay in Jester, just as they'd planned ten years ago.

Better late than never.

As he slowed the pickup for the turn onto the Cottonwood Farm road, he caught sight of bright red-and-black No Trespassing signs posted on the gate posts. Jennifer had followed his advice. If strangers showed up again, he'd have reason to arrest them and hold them for questioning, long enough at least to make sure they weren't a threat to any of the folks he was sworn to protect and serve.

The front of the old farmhouse seemed bare with the one large tree missing, but Luke immediately forgot its absence at the sight of a strange car parked in front of the porch. Luke pulled behind the dark green, late-model Mercedes and noted the Illinois license plates.

No strangers, Jennifer had said. Luke took the front steps three at a time, wondering who the visitor could be, and knocked at the front door.

"Come in," Jennifer called in a voice that sounded strained, as if she were attempting to be pleasant. "We're in the living room."

We?

Luke stepped inside and entered the room. A tall, good-looking man with blond hair and pale gray eyes stood beside Jennifer.

"Luke," she said, "this is Brad Harrison, my boss from my old job in Chicago. Brad, Luke McNeil."

The man grinned like a toothpaste ad, offered his hand and pumped Luke's in a greeting. "Glad to meet you. You can be the first to hear our happy news.''

''What news?'' Jennifer demanded.

Harrison moved toward her and draped his arm around her shoulder in a proprietary gesture. ''That we're getting married.''

Luke felt the breath leave his lungs as if he'd been sucker-punched. ''Married.''

''No—'' Jennifer began, but Harrison cut her off.

''We'll sell the farm,'' he said, ''then move back to my place in Chicago.''

Luke forced his expression to remain impassive. After their night together during the ice storm, he would have sworn Jennifer loved him, but apparently she'd been planning to marry Harrison all along.

''Congratulations.'' Luke forced the word through stiff lips. ''Now if that's all you had to say, I have work to do.''

Jennifer wrenched herself from Harrison's grip. ''But it isn't—''

''You don't owe me any explanation,'' Luke said.

Harrison merely grinned like a man who'd won the lottery. Which, in effect, he had. Third-hand.

Luke was already at the front door when Jennifer's call stopped him.

''Sheriff McNeil!''

Luke turned to find her standing in the doorway to the living room. ''Yes?''

"This man is trespassing. I've asked him to leave and he won't go. I need your help."

Luke could read the pleading in her eyes. "You're sure?"

"But, Jennifer, sweetheart—" Harrison whined behind her.

"I am not now nor have I ever been your sweetheart, Brad. Now for the last time, please get out of my house and off my property."

With a shrug of resignation, Harrison picked up an expensive cashmere overcoat from the rack in the hall. "Don't you even want to hear what my appraisers found out?"

Jennifer's eyes narrowed. "Appraisers?"

"Property appraisers. I sent a couple of them out to assess the value of your farm."

Bingo, Luke thought. That explained the strange men in the black Expedition.

"You had no right to do that," Jennifer said hotly, her cheeks glowing a mesmerizing pink.

"With the sale of the farm and the investment of your inheritance," Harrison said, "we'll be set for life."

"There's one little thing you've never mentioned," she replied in a cutting tone, "not that it would make any difference."

Harrison looked puzzled. "What's that?"

"Love," Jennifer said, and the look she turned on Luke was filled with so much love it took his breath away.

He turned and opened the door. "Your car's waiting, Harrison. If you're not off the property in five minutes, you'll be under arrest."

"I came as soon as I could after you quit to come out here." Harrison rammed his arms into his coat and glared at Jennifer. "You'll be sorry you passed up a catch like me."

"I'll take my chances," she said with a grimace of disgust.

Harrison stormed out the door and slammed it behind him. Jennifer threw herself into Luke's arms, and he'd never known another human being could feel so good.

"Was Harrison why you called me?" he asked, his lips against her hair.

She shook her head. "He showed up right before you arrived. He was always full of himself. I guess he thought I'd keel over with gratitude at his proposal."

Luke leaned back and gazed into her eyes. "You weren't tempted?"

Jennifer shuddered. "The man's too much in love with himself ever to love anyone else. I'm glad you were here to get rid of him."

Luke hugged her again. 'Me, too." He held her for a few delicious moments, drinking in her warmth and the fragrance of roses. "Why did you call me?"

"I wanted to show you something." Jennifer

pulled away, took his hand and led him to her grand-parents' bedroom. "I was going through Gramma's things this morning and discovered this."

She pulled open the top drawer of the dressing table. There, nestled atop a pile of neatly folded silk scarves, was an envelope, yellow with age and ad-dressed to Luke in Jennifer's handwriting.

"I did write you, Luke. It's right where Grandpa must have dropped it, then forgotten it. I doubt he ever opened that drawer again after I left."

Luke reached for the envelope. "May I read it?"

She nodded. "It's addressed to you."

Luke tore open the envelope and removed two sheets of paper covered in tearstained ink. His own eyes filled with tears as he read the heartrending letter Jennifer had written a decade earlier. Her hurt and confusion at her grandfather's banishment were evident, but what came through loud and clear was her love for Luke and her plea for him to contact her so they could make their plans.

She hadn't lied about leaving him a message, and he cursed the misunderstanding that had kept them apart.

He dropped the letter on the dressing table and drew her into his arms. "I love you, Jennifer. I can't believe the time we've wasted."

His lips sought hers and she melded to him in a kiss that held the promise of so much more.

"I love you, too, Luke."

He studied her face, but all he found was love shining through. No deception. No lies. Only the truth of her feelings for him.

"Marry me, Jenny. I earn enough to support a family, and if you want to raise them here on Cottonwood Farm, we can do that."

"We don't have to worry about money," she said with a laugh. "Have you forgotten I'm a millionaire?"

"We'll need that for the kids' college," he said solemnly. "You wanted a big family, remember?"

She flung her arms around his neck, and he lifted her and whirled her around the room.

"Oh, yes, Luke. I remember everything. But most of all, how much I love you."

* * * * *

*Find out what happens when one of the
Main Street Millionaires has to marry
his enemy in the next installment of*
MILLIONAIRE, MONTANA.
Don't miss

FOUR-KARAT FIANCÉE

*by Sharon Swan,
available in April 2003.
Only from Harlequin American Romance.*

HARLEQUIN®

AMERICAN *Romance*®

Celebrating 20 Years
of home, heart and happiness!

As part of our yearlong 20th Anniversary celebration,
Harlequin American Romance is launching a brand-new
cover look this April. And, in the coming months,
we'll be bringing back some of your favorite
authors and miniseries. Don't miss:

THAT SUMMER IN MAINE
by Muriel Jensen

A heartwarming story of unexpected
second chances, available in April 2003.

SAVED BY A TEXAS-SIZED WEDDING
by Judy Christenberry

Another story in Judy's bestselling
Tots for Texans series, available in May 2003.

TAKING OVER THE TYCOON
by Cathy Gillen Thacker

A spin-off story from Cathy's series,
The Deveraux Legacy, available in June 2003.

We've got a stellar lineup for you all year long,
so join in the celebration and enjoy
all Harlequin American Romance has to offer.

Available at your favorite retail outlet.

HARLEQUIN®
Live the emotion™

Visit us at www.eHarlequin.com

HARTAC2

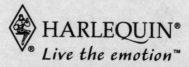

A "Mother of the Year" contest brings overwhelming response as thousands of women vie for the luxurious grand prize....

Kate Hoffmann

Jacqueline Diamond

Jill Shalvis

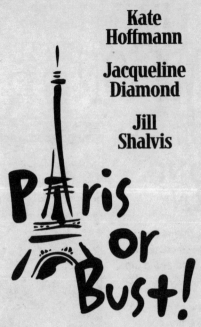

Paris or Bust!

A hilarious and romantic trio of new stories!

With a trip to Paris at stake, these women are determined to win! But the laughs are many as three of them discover that being finalists isn't the most excitement they'll ever have.... Falling in love is!

Available in April 2003.

HARLEQUIN®
Makes any time special ®

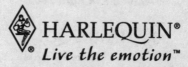